BUCK

Heroic dog story of Adventure, struggle & love

SHIRLEE LAWRENCE-VERPLOEGEN

authorHOUSE

AuthorHouse™
1663 Liberty Drive
Bloomington, IN 47403
www.authorhouse.com
Phone: 1 (800) 839-8640

© 2019 Shirlee Lawrence-Verploegen. All rights reserved.

No part of this book may be reproduced, stored in a retrieval system, or transmitted by any means without the written permission of the author.

Published by AuthorHouse 11/15/2019

ISBN: 978-1-7283-3551-3 (sc)
ISBN: 978-1-7283-3552-0 (hc)
ISBN: 978-1-7283-3550-6 (e)

Print information available on the last page.

Any people depicted in stock imagery provided by Getty Images are models, and such images are being used for illustrative purposes only.
Certain stock imagery © Getty Images.

This book is printed on acid-free paper.

Because of the dynamic nature of the Internet, any web addresses or links contained in this book may have changed since publication and may no longer be valid. The views expressed in this work are solely those of the author and do not necessarily reflect the views of the publisher, and the publisher hereby disclaims any responsibility for them.

Contents

Introduction vii
Prologue ix

Buck and the Browns 1
Mom, the Boys, and Willie 11
Buck, Jake, and Floodwater 15
Chickens, Voles, and Lyman, Mississippi 19
Teddy and the Eastern Diamondback Rattlesnake 27
Sore Pads and Thievery in Saucier 33
Wilma Witherspoon in McHenry, Mississippi 39
Bonding with Buck 45
Mrs. Witherspoon's Agenda 49
Mississippi Chinese 53
Grandma, Please, One More Story 59
Cozy as a Bedbug in McHenry 63
The Witherspoon Cotton Plantation 67
How the Boll Weevil Got to Mississippi 73
The End of Harvest Brings Bad News 77
The Green Dragon 81
On the Road Again 87

The Academy 91
Graduation from the Academy 109
A Quiet Celebration..113
Hoss Makes the Headlines 121
The Boys Hear About It Too 125
Searching for Answers 129
Dear John Phone Calls..135
The Beat..141
The Raid 145
Anxiety in Houston 149
Good News for Amy 151
Dolly...155
The Brown Family Comes to Houston 157
What About Jake..163
Jake 167
Putting Jake to Rest..173
Blessed Be the Grandfather...179
Giving Back?..181

Author's Notes..185
References...191
Free Preview 193
About the Author...205

Introduction

Allow me to introduce you to Buck, a beloved pet dog owned by a rural family in Louisiana. Buck is the main character in this story, and he entertains a multitude of people who pass through his life during the somewhat endless journey to survive hurricane Katrina and find a forever home. The Brown family's lives are also about to be turned upside down and filled with unforeseen challenge and misery. The onset of a category-five hurricane changes the lives of thousands of people and animals in the immediate area of Louisiana and Mississippi. During this time, pets are not accepted in shelters; so many animals are either left behind or become naturally lost and homeless. Buck is no exception. His struggle for survival exemplifies the strength of a hero who takes on a storybook journey. He moves from starving and wounded to leading the pack—a bonded collection of Buck and two additional homeless pups who need his wisdom and leadership. There are humorous times as these three amigos get into lots of trouble, always looking for food and a better place. This journey gives Buck numerous temporary owners, each one with its own unique story and challenges. You might say Buck becomes notorious for the love of adventure and becomes good at it—almost famous. He even takes on a new profession using his discipline and intellect. During all of this drama with Buck, the Brown family has their own share of change in their lives. Come with me as we move through the South, which is entrenched in so much rich history that intertwines within the story, making it as realistic as being there.

Prologue

It was August 24, 2005, and everyone on the Gulf Coast was staying close to the news. Hurricane Katrina was due to hit South Florida tomorrow. It was a category-five hurricane now in the Caribbean.

The general population in this area was accustomed to experiencing the routine of hurricane warnings and watches. Some people evacuated, and some chose to stay for various reasons. A certain percentage of the population in this region lacked transportation or did not have the money to travel or a place to go to. This time, however, qualified for more serious attention, as damage was expected along a wide stretch of the Gulf Coast, including Florida, Louisiana, and Mississippi.

There was the usual run on the grocery stores to stock up on supplies of bottled water and staples. Hardware stores and household discounters were selling all their supplies of plywood, sand, and other necessities to board up windows and dam for flooding. It was a busy time for all, and almost everyone was on edge.

As predicted, Katrina hit Florida on August 25 at 6:10 p.m. At this point, Katrina had moved down to a category-two storm. Next New Orleans and other parts of the Gulf Coast were bracing for the storm. The mayor of New Orleans was concerned about flooding and the possibility of the levees breaching, which could allow fifteen to twenty feet of water to inundate some parts of the city. Much of New Orleans is up to twelve feet below sea level and protected by a series of levees, channels, and pump stations. The Mississippi River winds its way through the city and carries about a third of the runoff of the continental United States.

With the hurricane now in the warm waters of the gulf, it was growing in intensity and showing signs that it would hit with more severity the next time. It so happened that the people of New Orleans had three days to prepare for Katrina to make landfall after the storm moved over the Florida peninsula.

Hurricane Katrina hit New Orleans on August 29 at 6:10 p.m. It had grown to a category-three plus storm when it made landfall. There was mass mayhem, as many people (mostly the old, sick, and poor populations) had not evacuated and were caught in the most destructive disaster the city had ever encountered. Levees overtopped at 8:00 a.m. on the twenty-ninth.

While overtopping some major levees in New Orleans, Katrina inundated most of the Louisiana and Mississippi coasts with up to twenty-foot storm surges. When the storm came ashore Monday morning, winds were topping 140 mph and transforming street signs, tree branches, and roof debris into projectiles.

The Alabama National Guard activated 450 troops to secure the city of Mobile and activated battalions of about 800 troops that were allocated to assist in Mississippi as needed. By now search-and-rescue missions were under way in the coastal counties of Mississippi. In Mobile, Alabama, the storm pushed Mobile Bay into downtown, submerging large sections of the city, and officials imposed a dusk-to-dawn curfew. Looting was reported by police in Gulfport, Mississippi, where the storm surge left downtown streets under ten feet of water. The downtown of Biloxi, Mississippi, which is located on a peninsula between the Gulf Coast and the Back Bay, was almost totally destroyed near the coastal areas.

Katrina's outer bands spawned tornadoes in Georgia on Monday evening. Three twisters were reported in Georgia. Officials were encouraging people who evacuated not to come back to southern Georgia for at least a week.

Hurricane Katrina left over fifty people dead Monday, almost all of them in one Mississippi County. More than seventy-five thousand people were being housed in almost 250 shelters across the region. In response, The American Red Cross launched the largest relief operation in its history for this disaster. The situation appeared to be getting worse hour by hour with no relief in sight.

On Monday evening, more than twelve hours after making landfall east of New Orleans, Katrina was finally downgraded to a tropical storm with winds of 60 mph. It then headed toward Tennessee and the Ohio River Valley, causing flooding in low-lying areas.

The ferocity of Hurricane Katrina etched the date August 29, 2005, in the minds of everyone who experienced it. South Mississippians, and the thousands of people from across the country who came to their aid, were forever shaped by the disaster and its aftermath.

Let's Not Forget the Animals

Many people would not leave their homes because they could not take their pets. Many people wanted to leave with rescue workers; but learning that their animals would not be accepted in the safe centers, decided to stay with their animals.

Courageous rescuers fought to save the lives of animals right after Katrina, but so many animals suffered and died anyway.

There are endless chronicles of volunteer efforts to rescue pets left in peril after their owners fled Katrina. The owners were then prevented from returning to some areas for long periods.

The plight of thousands of animals who perished in the floods, or who waited hour after hour, day after day, for owners or help that never arrived has been documented.

Some were trapped in homes or braved the toxic streets. Most were turned away from the shelters, as the shelters could take in only people. Some were separated from their owners before the storm and never made it home. There are many more scenarios—more than one can count. The basic truth is that we failed them.

No one can stop a category-five storm from ravaging a city, but our failure at every level to plan for evacuation ahead of time and have adequate response to the chaos and crisis afterward resulted in needless death and the prolonged anguish of both humans and animals.

Despite the odds, and with little regard for their personal safety or comfort, animal rescuers worked from dawn until long past dark for over six weeks to meet the need.

Chapter 1

Buck and the Browns

Just north of Highway 90 and west of Gulfport, Mississippi, the Brown family lived in a modest two-bedroom prefabricated home on a lot with numerous trees and privacy. Highway 90 ran along the shore of the Gulf of Mexico in this part of the Mississippi coast. It was a fairly rural setting, but houses were close by.

Mr. Jake Brown worked for a local lumber mill and walked to work every day, as it was less than two miles, so he could leave the family pickup home. Jake had lost his driver's license the previous year for driving while intoxicated. His dog, Buck, always accompanied him on the walk to work and sometimes would hang around the lumber mill. The dog wandered around the area, sniffing out whatever the day brought his way. Buck would end up at the lumber mill in the late afternoon to wait for his master so they could walk home together.

Mrs. Trudy Brown, a homemaker, stayed busy caring for her two children, Zack and Ben. Jake and Trudy had come to the area five years before, when friends said there was a good job for Jake at the mill. Times were hard for the Browns, as Jake was not very well educated and had to move around where work was available.

They had, since moving to the South, experienced many storms that frequented the area; but they, like many others, had never left their home. They also didn't realize the severity of the storm that was approaching and the fact that their lives were in such serious danger.

This time, however, after the storm hit Florida on Thursday, August 25, and was heading their way, the community was abuzz. Talk was all about the probability of the hurricane bringing widespread destruction. Most of the Browns' neighbors, and many of the families whose men worked at the mill with Jake, were already planning to evacuate. Unfortunately, Jake was not one of them.

Ben, the twelve-year-old, kept repeating to his mom what he was hearing on television about Hurricane Katrina warnings. He wondered about the differences between a tropical disturbance, a tropical storm, and a hurricane. He was absorbed in finding out more about Katrina. School had been dismissed all week.

Ben went next door to see if Mrs. Sperry would let him search the computer for more information. He often used their computer for school projects. When he knocked on her door on Friday, she was moving items from downstairs to upstairs and packing bags for the trip north to her sister's house in Memphis. She allowed him to use the computer, all the while ranting that there was no question as to whether to evacuate or not and that he'd better talk to his mom and dad. Mr. and Mrs. Sperry liked Ben and Zack, who was five, and interacted with them often. They did not, however, care much for the boys' parents, who seemed distant and dysfunctional.

Ben found on CNN.com that a tropical disturbance was created when tropical depressions headed for the southern United States began over warm ocean waters off the west coast of Africa. Massive thunderstorms took the warm air from the surface of the water and pushed it up until it cooled and came back down. Over and over this happened, causing the atmospheric pressure to change and creating vertical systems with a maximum wind speed of thirty-eight miles per hour over the ocean. Of the eighty to one hundred systems that developed throughout the season, only about ten became tropical storms that crossed the southern Atlantic.

Ben's interest was piqued as he read on.

A tropical depression became a tropical storm when winds reached thirty-nine miles per hour. The storm was then given an official name. Tropical storms were capable of breaking tree branches, tipping over lightweight trucks, damaging poorly built buildings, and causing high ocean waves and flooding. He remembered several times when his family had experienced tropical storms and afterward cleaned up the fallen tree branches and other debris. They always scared him and Zack. Usually Ben, Zack, and Buck would all get into one bed and huddle together until it was over.

It was the next information that terrified Ben. He had never actually read a description of storms like this before. He certainly had never experienced one.

When winds hit seventy-four miles per hour, a tropical storm took a cyclonic form and became a *hurricane*. With its strongest winds in the right-front quadrant, a hurricane produced swirls of foam and spray on the water and reduced visibility. Winds could inflict moderate to heavy damage on structures and trees, and flooding could occur. Severity was measured on a scale of one to five. The deadliest hurricane in US history, a category four by today's standards, killed eight thousand people in Galveston, Texas, in 1900.

Ben experienced a knot in his stomach. He'd heard on television that Hurricane Katrina was supposed to be one of the biggest, most damaging storms the area had ever experienced. He printed the material, said goodbye to Mrs. Sperry, and ran home with sweat forming on his brow. No wonder the schools had closed and all the fervor around him seemed wild and frantic! There was a chance they would die if they didn't evacuate! But where would they go? The only relatives he knew of were his grandparents on his mother's side, but they lived someplace in Kentucky and rarely communicated. Ben wondered if it was possible to go there.

It didn't seem too unusual to Ben or Zack that their family never had visits or phone calls from other family members. It had always been that way, except for the one time when Ben was a young boy and his family lived with the grandparents for a short time. He *did* know that the grandparents did not approve of his dad. They often told his mother, "Jake is no good." They encouraged Trudy to leave him, but she was a meek and insecure woman who had married young and felt as if she were in a helpless situation. She believed she could not make it on her own.

Ben's whole life had been lacking healthy family interaction. He and Zack never got cards from their grandparents on their birthdays or special occasions. The truth was that his own mom and dad never celebrated much of anything. There was a lack of communication among his family members. They would even spend Christmas at home in a low-key manner.

Everyone in the family feared Ben's father, and his mother just clammed up when Jake would come home drunk for fear he would give her another black eye. He never bothered the boys, however—just their mom. He took out bad days on her and blamed her for everything.

In fact, Jake acted as if the boys were just a nuisance to be around. After supper, family members always stayed out of his way and remained quiet until bedtime.

Buck was the only one who seemed to get along with everybody. He was Jake's only friend and was the boys' best buddy. He spent his days with Jake and his evenings with the boys.

With tears in his eyes, Ben ran from the Sperry's home to find his mom. He seemed in a panic to explain what might happen to them. He showed her the printed material and was talking fast. Trudy had finished only the ninth grade and had difficulty understanding the material. She told Ben he had to talk with his dad when he got home. Ben felt empty because he knew it was almost impossible to communicate with his dad. Ben was terrified.

He ran upstairs and started pulling out clothes to take. He felt mentally frustrated and helpless. He was just going through the motions of grabbing a few things to keep his mind occupied. He thought of Buck and Zack, plus the two hamsters in the cage in his room. He had never been so distraught and felt almost sick to his stomach. He knew his dad could act belligerent and mean at times. Jake never listened to anyone in the family. All he cared about after work was his bottle of whiskey.

Ben's mother constantly brought up the fact that if Jake didn't spend so much on liquor and worked harder, the family could have a better life. Jake's drinking had worsened every year. His only friend was Buck, who remained steadfast in his loyalty. Rarely did Buck have to experience anger or abuse from him.

Jake walked home about 6:30 p.m. on that Friday night while drinking his whiskey and talking to Buck, who always listened. He came into the house and plopped on the couch in front of the television, even though he didn't watch it.

Ben had been waiting and went into the room to talk with his dad. He told him about Katrina and what he had found out that day on the computer. His dad just looked at him with fuzzy eyes and said, "Now, Ben, you can't always believe what you hear on television. I've been through a lot of storms. It's just like all the others; we will be okay."

Ben explained that Mrs. Sperry's family was packing to evacuate, and from all indications they would be in serious trouble if they didn't leave. His dad just said, "Go find your mom and find out what's for supper. Tell her me and Buck is hungry."

Trudy came from the kitchen and announced that tonight's dinner was beans and rice along with hoecakes, and she added that everything was ready. She asked Jake about what Ben had found out and asked if she should make arrangements for them to leave. He looked daggers at her and said, "If I hear one more thing about this gall-darned storm, I'm going to kick ass and take names. Bring me my supper."

That night they ate in silence around the couch and on the floor. They never sat down to the table for their evening meal. That would have meant facing each other and possibly talking to one another. After supper, Jake noticed that his whiskey bottle had one more drink left in it, so he polished it off. He then fell back on the sofa and dropped into a stuporous sleep, snoring like a bull moose. Buck decided it was more than he could take and went with Ben to his bedroom. He and Ben curled up together in bed.

Ben was unable to go to sleep, and Buck sensed something was wrong. He lay still, keeping his eyes on Ben for a long time. Buck had a way of lying still with his eyes open like a gator. His eyes could move around, watching whatever movement was going on around him, but his head remained down. When Ben hugged Buck and kissed him on the head, Buck licked Ben all over his face and hands and then finally closed his eyes to sleep. They could hear the hamsters stirring in the cage. Ben's mind was racing, and he was scared. He quietly cried and hugged Buck even closer.

Ben and Buck shared a lot together. On weekends, they went fishing and had many adventures playing pirates, hunting for treasure, and chasing rabbits and squirrels. Ben sometimes thought Buck was his only friend. He had no close friends from school, as he felt he didn't fit in. Some of the kids made fun of his clothes. He always wore used clothes from Goodwill or the Salvation Army. His backpack was even a threadbare replica of some off brand; the zippers were stubborn, and he feared they would break any day and his books would come falling out. That would give them all something else to laugh about at school.

Ben was a good student, however. He especially liked geography and history. He had become proficient in researching subjects on the computer to write good papers to turn in. He liked going to school, except for the kids who teased him. It was better than being home.

Zack had always been a mama's boy and clung to her like a baby opossum. Zack and his mother cleaned up the kitchen and left Dad on the sofa to sleep. They went to bed together, and as usual, sad tears flowed down Trudy's face while she hugged up to Zack in bed. Life was a struggle every day, and today was no different.

The next day, Jake was told that the mill would be closing the following day until further notice because so many workers were leaving town to avoid the upcoming storm. As Jake had said he wasn't leaving, his supervisor told him that if he wanted to come in to help secure the building the next day, it would be appreciated. They spent the present day preparing for the mill to close and doing what they could to protect the lumber and machinery. The building was boarded up. Only a few things were left for Jake to finish the next day to close down the facility.

That night, Jake was drunk even before he got home. He had stopped off at his local whiskey contact's house and talked to what locals were left. Most of them were like him—heavy drinkers who were not thinking clearly. He fell twice while walking home, swearing under his breath about the rain and whatever was in his way. Buck tagged along dutifully, used to the drunken banter.

When Jake got home, Ben once again started begging his dad to help make plans to evacuate the house, but as on the night before, his dad did not listen or seem to care. Ben had been working on his mother all day to leave without Dad if he wouldn't go. He assured her they could come back later and check on Dad after the storm. Trudy had not responded positively but was secretly was toying with the idea of leaving after Jake left the next morning.

The next day, Jake helped with last-minute details to close down the mill. Buck went along as always but was frustrated with the wind and rain they had endured to get to the mill. He had a thick coat of fur, and when he was soaking wet, he felt heavy. Instead of wandering through the woods that day chasing squirrels and rabbits, he curled up by the door to the office and waited for his owner to finish work. He did his best to stay out of the rain and get dry, but the torrential force of the rain and wind was too challenging.

Ben had finally convinced his mother to evacuate—take the truck and just leave until the storm was over. There was one problem, however, with Ben. He was crying because he could not bear the thought of leaving Buck. He begged Mom just to ride by the mill and pick him up. Trudy explained that if they gave any hint that they were leaving, the plan could fall through. Ben even begged her to let him run the two miles to the mill and coax Buck back without Dad knowing about it. She wouldn't listen, so they filled the back of the truck with a few belongings, including the hamsters, secured the top with a tarp, piled into the old truck, and headed north. Ben sobbed for at least an hour until all his tears ran dry. He wanted Buck and feared for his safety. He sat silent in the truck, numb with grief and scared of the storm already pounding on the truck.

He thought of the evening on which Dad had brought Buck home almost two years before. Buck was a ball of fur about six weeks old. One of the men at the mill had let Jake pick him out of a new litter of puppies. Buck missed his mommy the first few nights, but he fell fast in love with the family. He was about a year old when Jake started taking him along every day on the walk to the mill. Now Buck was about two years old. He was a beautiful dog of about fifty-five pounds with a thick coat of brindle-colored fur. Buck looked like an Australian cattle dog with the somewhat threatening face of a German shepherd. He was anything but threatening, however, as most people who knew him would tell you. He was an adventure-bound, loving, and loyal dog.

Trudy didn't know where they were going and had less than twenty dollars. The gas tank showed half full; she only hoped they could find shelter somewhere along the way before the gas ran out. She had packed some biscuits with beans to tide them over. They drove for hours through thick sheets of rain, and wind that moved the truck from side to side. All of them were on the edge of their seat, their eyes glued to the windshield. Travel was very slow, and the tension was high. Trudy worried about facing Jake after going against his wishes and leaving. She knew it wouldn't be good. Trudy knew he would be furious with her; she considered that maybe she just wouldn't go back at all. She thought that when she could get everyone stable, maybe she could call her parents and they would help.

Jake was done at the mill, and he and Buck headed home. They stopped first at the house of a man who had always furnished the local community with moonshine. He had locked his house and left. Jake always made his daily trip by there, and he was furious. He began breaking windows, kicking at the door, and spewing out unpleasant swear words. Buck was a little anxious and very confused at what was happening.

After a few minutes, they headed home in the rain. It was raining so hard that they had great difficulty walking and seeing clearly. The wind pushed both of them around as they walked, and both Jake and Buck began to be fearful of the weather. Jake thought about Ben begging him to evacuate, and Buck thought about Ben coaxing him to stay home this morning. Jake had insisted Buck come along with him to the mill as always.

After about ten minutes of struggling through the wind and rain, Jake decided to go back to the mill until the worst part of the storm blew over. He and Buck turned around and fought their way back to safety.

When they arrived, Jake jimmied a lock to get shelter in one of offices. For hours, they just sat quietly and observed the storm. Soaked, cold, and hungry, Jake and Buck finally hunkered down for the night.

Later that night, Jake felt sick to his stomach and threw up; he swore under his breath. He pretty much felt like a freight train had run over him. He was shivering and shaky and wasn't thinking clearly either. He needed a drink to numb the pain.

Buck was very concerned about him and tried to remain close enough to offer some comfort and warmth. They were both pretty miserable. Buck thought about supper at home and Ben's warm bed, but something told him he needed to stay with his master.

During the night, hurricane-force winds reached coastal Mississippi and lasted over seventeen hours. Flooding started inland from the coast. Jake and Buck didn't know it, but the sixteen miles inland of their location could have been flooded at any time.

That night was scary. Close to morning, Jake could hear trees cracking and branches falling, as well as items sailing through the air and hitting the building. Several windows broke out, and the wind was bringing in items from the outside. Jake and Buck moved several times to safer areas of the room. It sounded as if the roof was going to come off at any moment. Instead of the storm subsiding, it seemed to get worse. They stayed in the building till midmorning, waiting for a break.

Mom, the Boys, and Willie

In the meantime, Mom, Zack, and Ben had traveled about seventy-five miles north to Hattiesburg, Mississippi. They were one family among many looking for shelter. They ended up in a Baptist church, where they slept on cots, had a warm meal, and were able to stay together. Trudy and Ben told one of the people in charge all about Dad and Buck being left behind and how worried they were about their safety. The people managing the shelter said they would do what they could through the Red Cross to find out something. In the meantime, the church volunteers encouraged them to pray for Dad and Buck and to thank God for being saved from perishing in the hurricane. That is all they had to hang on to, and so day after day went by without any word, and the praying continued. After a few days, more supplies were brought in for the stranded; they were able to clean up and feel a little better.

This church often took in the indigent and was set up for managing people in need. The food was better than the Browns were accustomed to, and both Zack and Ben ate heartily. They even sneaked apples back to their cots to hide for later. The hamsters were kept in another area but were safe and cared for. The boys would eat their apples and then take the cores to the hamsters, which foraged enthusiastically on them.

All was somewhat well except for the fears about Dad and Buck. Even though Dad had not been a loving and caring father, everyone still cared about him and hoped for the best.

By 4:30 a.m., just hours before Hurricane Katrina made landfall, many shelters in Mississippi were full to capacity, including many Red Cross Shelters, the Jackson Mississippi Coliseum, and five special-needs shelters. The shelters had filled within twenty-four hours of opening.

Everyone at the shelter weathered the storm, trying to stay busy and tuning in to any news coming in. They heard that people were not able to go back home yet. The destruction was great.

When electricity was restored to the area, Trudy finally connected with her mom and dad, and her parents consented for them to come up to Kentucky whenever they could make it. Everything right now was on hold, as transportation was unstable. The family had only an old truck with no gas in it, and the buses were not running normally, if at all.

Within the shelter, Ben and Zack had made friends with an old man, Willie Chitto, who said his Mississippi descendants were Choctaw Indians. The old man had a calming effect on the boys and told them stories. Ben asked Willie to tell him more about the Indians, and the old man seemed pleased. He commenced to tell the Mississippi story of the Choctaws going back to as early as 1700.

Willie said the Choctaws were the largest and strongest tribe in Mississippi, and while they had endured much strife over the years, they were now one of the state's largest employers. Ben asked him more about the strife part.

He explained that the Indians prospered in trade and farming until the end of the eighteenth century, when the federal government acquired much of their land. It was Thomas Jefferson who issued military strategy to take all the lands bordering the east side of the Mississippi River for the purpose of defense. Under pressure, the Choctaws signed the Treaty of Fort Adams, ceding 2,641,920 acres of land from the Yazoo River to the thirty-first parallel. That was only the first of several treaties in which land was ceded to the government.

When the Treaty of Dancing Rabbit Creek was signed, approximately thirteen thousand Choctaws were removed to the West. More followed over the years. Those who chose to stay in Mississippi were their descendants, just like Willie Chitto.

Ben asked where the Indians were today and whether they lived on reservations and in tepees? Willie smiled, patted him on the head, and explained that the Indians today were businesspeople and that many did still live on reservations. The reservations did not look like they had in the past, just as all Mississippi towns now looked different. Everyone lived in houses with all the conveniences of modern life.

Ben asked what happened after they lost so much land. Willie said, "This is when the Choctaws went through some hard times." There were limited choices for their futures. The Choctaws worked primarily as sharecroppers, with little access to education or basic health care. There was no recognized tribal government.

Finally, in 1918 the US Congress investigated the living conditions of the Choctaws, who were living in the poorest pocket of poverty in the poorest state in the country. The Bureau of Indian Affairs established the Choctaw Indian Agency at Philadelphia, Mississippi, and addressed schools, health, and living conditions.

Willie proudly reported that his ancestor, Joe Chitto, was elected the first chairman of an official council, to look after the welfare of the tribal community. Unemployment at this time among the tribal community was a staggering 80 percent.

The council worked on many things that eventually brought about improved housing, skills training, and job opportunities. Many manufacturers were moving production to the South, where the workforce was not heavily unionized. One of the first manufacturers that came was Packard Electric, a division of General Motors. The Indians made wiring harnesses for cars on the reservation. Others followed, such as American Greetings, Caterpillar, Ford Power Products, and more.

Next came the tribe's most ambitious development. The US Congress passed the National Indian Gaming Act in 1988. It allowed tribes to operate casinos on reservations. The first casino, the Silver Star, was a springboard into the tourism industry.

Revenue from the tribe's business ventures enabled the tribe to build up its social and health care services, build schools and day care centers, and provide postsecondary education for its members. Economic success also strengthened the traditions and cultures of the Choctaw community. The Choctaw language is still spoken by most adults on the reservation, but younger tribal members are less likely to be fluent in the language.

Ben was in awe of Willie and his story. Willie had calmed Zack into a deep sleep in his lap. Trudy smiled as she watched the boys and their new friend.

Buck, Jake, and Floodwater

Finally, after the worst of the storm, Jake and Buck left the building in ankle-deep water. Less than ten minutes later, the streets were gushing with floodwater deeper than they could stand up in. The current carried them along, gasping for air and looking for something to grab onto.

Buck and Jake could swim, but they floundered in the water like rag dolls. Buck was traumatized and kept looking around for his master as he was carried along in the water. Jake had grabbed onto a tree and was hanging on for dear life. He watched Buck go downstream with the current, unable to do anything about it. Jake was weak and hysterical as he clung with all his strength to the tree and wondered for the first time about his family. His dog was gone, and now he was all alone.

Jake hung on for about four hours before someone in a boat came along and tried to pull him from the water. In trying to get him aboard, the boat capsized, and all three men fell into the water. They managed to grab the boat, haul themselves back inside, and finally get Jake inside as well. Jake was sick, cold, weak, and exhausted. They moved on to get some medical assistance for Jake and continue watching for other flood victims. Jake lay dazed in the boat, shivering and somewhat delirious.

Buck swam among the rushing water and was swept along by the current for a long time until he found a piece of wood to pull himself onto. He was exhausted and coughed up a lot of water. Buck tried to keep his balance on the piece of wood for as long as he could. I am sure it was hours, but for Buck it seemed like a lifetime. He traveled at least five or six miles down the flood creek and finally came to a patch of higher ground that the wood ran aground upon. At this point, Buck and his wobbly legs came ashore, and he wondered what to do next. All he could do at the moment was lie down, rest, and try to regain his strength.

Jake was taken to a local and temporary medical facility, checked over, and allowed to rest until his strength came back. He was fed bread and jam, water, and dried fruit, and he seemed to feel a little stronger within a few hours. The problem was that his need for alcohol was kicking in with a vengeance, and he had stomach cramps, nausea, and almost hallucinatory thoughts of bugs and other unpleasant things crawling on him. He was experiencing delirium tremens, or DTs; people with alcohol dependency are all familiar with these symptoms.

He remained in the medical area and had to deal with this without much attention to his needs. There were too many other people who were missing or had been rescued with life-threatening issues for medical personnel to give Jake enough time to sort through his personal problems. He moved from the medical facility to a local shelter and began to get sicker, not only because of his physical issues but also because of his mental ones stemming from his having ignored his family. There was no power and no functional phone lines. The Brown family didn't have a phone at the house, so it was doubly frustrating. Everyone was talking about the devastation, the deaths, the floods, people stuck on roofs, and the general condition of the area.

Jake began to hear horror stories. For example, since the evacuation was not total, many people survived the thirty-foot storm tide by climbing into their second-floor attics, or by knocking out walls and ceiling boards to climb onto their roofs or into nearby trees. People had swum to taller buildings or trees. Many people were rescued from rooftops and trees in Mississippi. Possibly fewer people died in Mississippi during Hurricane Katrina. Jake hoped his family was not included in that number.

Jake decided he would try to make his way back home somehow. He gave up his spot at the shelter and started walking south, open to any idea to get back home that came along. He found out, unfortunately, that all traffic was blocked from going back into the area and there were no means to get there. He met up with some homeless people near a railroad and eagerly partook of some of their whiskey to settle his nerves. Jake was now a homeless alcoholic without support of any kind at the moment to aid his efforts to find his family. He buried himself in whiskey or whatever else he could beg, borrow, or steal. He slept with other nomads around the railroad and drowned his troubles in a bottle.

The Mississippi Gulf Coast had been devastated. The extent of the devastation throughout Mississippi was also staggering. Since Katrina hit, more than half a million people in Mississippi were in the process of applying for assistance from the Federal Emergency Management Agency (FEMA). In a state of just 2.9 million residents, that means more than one in six Mississippians sought help. More than ninety-seven thousand people are today still living in FEMA trailers and mobile homes. Another five thousand to six thousand are still waiting for FEMA trailers.

Surveying the damage the day after Katrina's passing, the Mississippi governor called the scene indescribable, saying "I can only imagine that is what Hiroshima looked like 60 years ago. This is our tsunami."

Most animal shelters in the area were destroyed. Pet enthusiasts developed portable shelters called "Camp Katrinas" to continue their rescue work to save animals.

Cities ran rampant with stray, sick, and malnourished animals. This was true even farther north, where the floodwaters were not so prevalent. One could drive along any street and see five or six dogs in a dead-end street, all looking traumatized and ill. Local authorities saw a growing need to clean up their cities, so they began to pick up the animals en masse every day. Unfortunately, these animals were put down.

Buck, too, was homeless and began his struggles and adventures to find refuge.

Chickens, Voles, and Lyman, Mississippi

Buck hobbled to find a rock formation with an overhang to get under and out of the worst part of the rain. He stayed there for only a little while. He observed the cuts on his paws after climbing onto land. For a long time, he lay on the patch of higher land, licking his cuts and grooming down his thick fur that was covered with mud and water. Buck's big eyes were bloodshot from the water and the stress. He looked rugged and felt exhausted and insecure.

He walked down as far as he could back in the direction of where he had been separated from his master, but he couldn't get a scent on anything as there was so much water everywhere. Not being able to understand what had happened or why, he began to walk among the trees and brush, looking for someone or something to break his thoughts of confusion.

It was still raining hard, but Buck walked for miles and came upon nothing but more trees and brush. He began to feel really lost and abandoned. He would lie down from time to time to rest his sore paws and lick them. Two places were bleeding, and the walking did not help his cuts. At least he was alive.

In northern Harrison County, Mississippi, where Buck was wandering, everything was rural and desolate. Farms and small communities were scattered throughout the county, but the distances between them were great, especially for a walking dog. At nightfall on the first night, Buck crawled under another overhanging rock and tried to make his body as small as possible to break the chill and get out of the rain. It was impossible, however, to stay dry. Mosquitoes and insects were a nuisance; Buck kept biting back at his tail, where the insects would land. He was a very frustrated and unhappy dog at this point. He was dripping wet, hungry, walking with sore paws in the rain, and fighting the insects.

At daybreak he started out again. After about three hours, Buck came upon the outskirts of the small community of Lyman, Mississippi. He saw a house with some smaller buildings around it and headed in that direction. Even though Lyman was only about six miles from where he washed ashore; wandering with no sense of direction in the pouring rain had taken him at least three times that distance.

As Buck got closer to the house, he noticed chickens strutting around the property, and drool began to drip from his mouth. He was really hungry. He had never killed a chicken, but he had chased loose chickens before at home. It was always a game—the chase—the chickens running, and Buck fast on their tails. It had been great fun, and some of those thoughts crossed his mind as he inched closer to the farm.

Buck slinked under the fence and made his way closer to the house, where the chickens were scratching and pecking the ground. He slowly moved in and, at the right moment, took off in a dead run after the chickens. At first he wasn't sure which one to concentrate on, as they were squawking with wings flapping and moving in all directions. It was also so muddy that he skidded down several times. Finally he was able to catch up to a pullet and bring her down.

At this point, he heard dogs barking in the house and a lot of commotion. The screen door to the house opened, and a farmer with his shotgun ran from the house toward Buck and the chickens. Buck felt scared and started to run. The farmer fired the shotgun several times at Buck. Buck was running for his life; he had never heard a shotgun before but knew the farmer's behavior and the sound were not good. As he was running, Buck felt the sting of many shotgun pellets hitting him. He fell once, got up, and continued to run into the nearest clump of trees. He continued to run for almost two miles before he noticed he was no longer being chased by the farmer. Buck had been pelted full of buckshot in his back and legs. He was in pain and found a muddy hole to lie in. Buck felt nauseated and threw up while he was licking his bloody wounds in the muddy water.

The rest of this day was spent hiding in the area; Buck's strength was sapped, and he was starving at this point. As dusk came and Buck lay in the hole, he saw two voles moving ahead of him along the grass. He gained enough strength to pounce on the area where the voles were. With his nose to the ground, he sniffed out two voles and ate them. He swallowed them whole. Buck would have preferred to kill the voles and eat them more slowly, but he couldn't risk the voles getting away from him. He needed food. It wasn't enough food to make a difference to Buck's stomach, but at least he began to feel a little better after the mini-meal and some success.

Buck was weak, and moving at all caused him pain. Reluctantly, he decided to find a bed for the night. Among the thickets, he felt a little more comfortable, as the rain was not hitting the ground with as much force as before. For the first time, he thought of Ben and the warm bed they shared each night. It seemed a distant memory.

As he lay in the thicket that night, he could hear all kinds of things that kept him alert and wondering. He had never slept outside before now. There seemed to be frequent movement in the thickets of varmints or insects coming out at night. He was tempted many times to forage for food again, but he didn't have the strength or the motivation to hunt in the dark.

From time to time, he could hear trucks and cars on a road in the distance. It was the darkest of darks, and Buck had never been in such a predicament.

Dogs' brains are about equivalent to the brain of a human at the toddler stage. They live for the moment and don't reason or make plans like older children and adults. This was a blessing for Buck during this time of grief, pain, and hunger. He did not think of dying in the same way as we might or wonder what was going to happen tomorrow. He only lay in his den for the night and tried to get as comfortable as possible with all his wounds and sleep a little. He never let his guard down, however, and was ready to jump at a moment's notice.

As light filtered into his den and he listened to the *drip drip* of raindrops falling on his head, Buck woke to a new day. He woke and lay there for a moment, trying to take in where he was and what to do next. He spent the better part of the next hour licking his wounds. The bleeding on his pads had stopped, but they were still tender. He could lick his legs where the shotgun pellets went into his skin, and he could twist around a little to reach a few places on his back. Most of the areas were bleeding. He was even able to chew at one place on his back leg, and one of the pellets came out. The spots were raw and sore. His weak feeling had not changed; he had not had enough food. As he struggled to move in the constant rain, he was reminded of his wounds.

Most people in this predicament would normally be admitted to the hospital for exhaustion, dehydration, near starvation, and treatment of injuries.

Even though Buck had been adopted by the Brown family when he was a pup, he had never been seriously mistreated or needed to fend for himself. However, he had a strong body and an equally strong will. He now had moved from a protected, comfortable life to survival.

Luckily Buck was still young enough to experience this type of adversity and still have the motivation to move on. His thick fur had been helpful to him during the rain, the cold and even the shotgun attack. After tending to his wounds, Buck wandered toward the sound of the trucks and cars on the road and soon found himself following the road north for about six blocks into Lyman. Lyman was just a wide place in the road, but it represented the community with a few stores and some commercial activity.

As Buck walked slowly toward the cluster of buildings, he saw people coming and going in cars and trucks, entering and exiting the buildings. He saw a few children playing around outside. He also saw two dogs lying on a stoop, looking timid and scared.

Buck decided to sit outside the building where most of the people were going inside. The children began to look at him with wide eyes, noticing the blood on his back and legs and the wet, muddy coat of hair with cockleburs in it. Buck lay down near the door and tried to appear friendlier. One girl came over and touched his head. He licked her hand. She stared at Buck with tears in her eyes and ran inside to tell her mom. The girl's mom came to the door and told her to stay away from the dog, as he could bite because he was injured. Buck looked up at the girl's mom with sad brown eyes, almost pleading for attention. The woman felt so bad for the dog that she went inside to talk to the shop owner. She wanted any meat scraps the man had and bought a box of dry dog food. She asked for a bowl of water. The man was very accommodating, and the woman moved about with a purpose to prepare to help the dog. She was mentally reminded that her family and pets had not been seriously damaged by the hurricane.

The woman came to the door like an angel from heaven with her arms full of food and water. She put it all down for Buck, careful not to touch him. She smiled and gave Buck her best wishes for getting better. She knew she had more important things to take care of at the moment; she couldn't do more. She and her daughter took their bags of groceries and drove away.

Buck ate as if there were no tomorrow. It was several minutes before he even looked up. He noticed that the two dogs from the stoop had crept over near him to watch him eat. He saw the shop owner looking out the window. He looked down at the food left and backed away for the other two dogs to eat. He then lay down nearby and watched them finish the food and water.

After a few minutes, the shop owner came out with a big stick and yelled at the dogs to disappear. He was aggressive in his movements and voice, so the dogs moved on down the street. The two small dogs followed behind Buck as if they had found a leader.

Lady was a blonde Pekingese that had lost her family. The family always tied her to a stake outside when they left the house. For some reason, the family had not returned. When the Hurricane came through, the incredibly high winds lifted Lady off the ground and swung her around the stake in the air. The rope broke, and Lady ran for cover. Hours later, she partnered with a neighbor dog, Teddy, and together they began to wander the area.

Teddy was a brown, black, and white Jack Russell terrier. He was feisty and fast. One wouldn't know that, though, with the way the dog was meandering along behind Buck. Teddy had floated on a rooftop with his family until they were rescued in a boat. The shelter would not take animals, so the parents had told the children Teddy would be better off fending for himself.

Now they were a pack of three very different dogs who shared the same dilemma—homelessness. They felt more comfortable together, but they had little in common as far as personality and appearance. One thing was for sure, though—Buck had become Lady and Teddy's big buddy. He had shared precious food with them: food that he could have kept for himself—food that he could have benefited from after not having eaten for three days. They all seemed to understand the situation; they followed him like a dad with two puppies down the stretch of road. Buck was glad to have company.

Buck was very hot and panting in the humid early September weather. His thick, dark coat held the heat, and his wounds could use some soothing. He led the dogs over to a large puddle of water, where they all lay together. Buck wallowed in the water to get his back covered. Lady and Teddy were not as crazy about being in the muddy water but dutifully stayed near Buck.

Teddy began to chase a honeybee; after eating, he was ready for action. He ran and jumped and tried his best to catch the bee in his mouth. Honeybees are Mississippi's official insect; they are common in the state. The bee was clumsy and gave Teddy a couple of chances, but somehow Teddy never connected. It was all for the better; Teddy didn't realize that he was playing with fire. Buck and Lady watched the entertainment from the cooling pool of water.

Lady had a sore neck from the rope burn that had rubbed off some of the hair on her neck. It was not serious, but she was happy just to rest. She moved closer to Buck, and he licked her neck. They were becoming fast friends. Buck's big pink tongue felt so good on her neck. Lady was a young dog of about ten months old. She liked the comforts of life and missed her family.

Teddy, on the other hand, was a rambunctious young man of one and one half years. He had springs in his feet and could jump as high as the sky. Jack Russells are notorious for their jumping and high energy levels. Teddy lived up to his name and was a cute bag of tricks just waiting to be opened. He lived for the moment and allowed life to be as fun as possible.

Buck decided to hang around Lyman; after all, he had gotten fed here. He kept his gator eyes on the door of the shop where he had eaten. The man had gone back inside, and occasionally someone would drive up and go into the shop. If Buck could avoid the man with the stick, he might get some sympathy from a passer-by—just as had happened before. For the moment, however, his belly was full, and he felt a comfort level come back that gave him more energy.

People would glance over at the three dogs as they entered and exited the area. No one stopped, however, to take a closer look or try to interact with them. Buck wondered if three was a crowd.

In the late afternoon, Buck wandered around the back of the buildings with Lady and Teddy close behind him. There were trash cans and stacks of cardboard boxes behind the shops.

Buck waited nearby until the activity of comings and goings died down. About dusk, when it appeared the shops were closed, he began checking out each trash can.

In the first one, he found oil cans and newspaper. There were several small plastic papers that had the smell of peanut butter on them. He licked them until the peanut butter was gone.

Teddy had already caught on and turned over the second can. He and Lady were sifting through trash, none of which held any food odors. Finally they joined Buck, who was rummaging through the third can, which belonged to the store. They found several pieces of bad fruit and two loaves of stale bread. The three dogs consumed the bread as though it were sirloin steak.

After dinner, Buck headed to the woods for shelter. Teddy and Lady looked at each other like, "Do we want to go into the woods?" and then ran fast to catch up. Buck walked and sniffed around for at least an hour. He ran several squirrels up trees and ended up at a bridge that was nearly covered in rushing water. It was several minutes before Teddy and Lady caught up to Buck. Teddy had stayed longer, chasing the squirrels, and Lady's short little legs just could not go as fast.

This area was officially a swamp. There are many swamps in and around Mississippi. Interspersed with major and minor streams, the large areas of swampland cannot drain, simply because they are as low as or lower than adjacent streams. This is a flood hazard. Over the ages, the land around these flood areas produced rich soil making Mississippi one of the most highly specialized cotton-growing sections of the world.

In the 1700s in this southern area of Mississippi, there were a few tribes of Indians: the Biloxis, Yazoos, and Pascagoulas, all of whom were weaker tribes than the Choctaws in the southeast and the Chickasaws in the north.

Buck crossed the small bridge, perusing the area. After some time, the three dogs came upon a campground area. This was located at the southernmost tip of the Desoto National Forest. The campground is fourteen miles from the Mississippi Gulf Coast, situated adjacent to the Big Biloxi River, where canoeing is a major activity.

Of course, there were no campers. Buck sniffed out all the grills in the campground. He finally decided the place was deserted and harmless. The three dogs bedded down inside the entry area of the restrooms, which had a covered roof. The corner served as a safe spot in which they could remain vigilant to anyone approaching.

Teddy found a spot to himself a few inches away from Buck and Lady. Lady lay close, touching Buck. Buck licked her neck, and Lady was appreciative. She returned the licks to Buck's face. Night and darkness surrounded them as they slept, tired from their day.

Teddy and the Eastern Diamondback Rattlesnake

The next morning, the three dogs woke one by one and sniffed out the area. Buck was the last one up. He took time to lick his wounds and ready his sore body for the day.

Lady was perched near a magnolia tree, doing her morning business. Teddy was running after a rabbit that had mistakenly ventured into the campground. Teddy was very vocal in his chase; there was no way to mistake the direction in which he entered the swampy forest. After losing the chase, he meandered back to the campground, looking for his friends.

All three of the dogs looked up as they noticed a park ranger driving his truck through the campground. They poised to run but stayed put near the area they had spent the night.

The park ranger circled the area and noticed the three dogs. His first thought was what an unlikely trio they made, and he then was reminded that many dogs were now homeless after the hurricane. He drove on and left the dogs alone without disturbing their morning. He had to be in town in a few minutes and didn't have time to fool with them.

Buck thought about heading back over to the store where they had eaten yesterday. He started into the woods, following his scent from the day before. Occasionally he would look back and notice Lady trotting dutifully along some distance behind. Teddy was always taking a lot of side trips left and right from the trail. His little legs were so fast that he could do this with ease and still keep up with his friends.

Buck found the small bridge and started across. He didn't notice the large snake lying on a rock just below. He continued his journey forward. Lady wasn't far behind. Teddy came across the bridge and saw the snake move. He naturally went to investigate the unusual creature. As Teddy approached the rock, the snake lay completely still at first and then began to put off a loud buzzing noise from his rattle. The snake was in a restful position but was bold looking and could be aggressive if he wanted to. The snake had a series of large brown diamonds outlined with cream-colored scales down to his tail. He had a somewhat masked face created by two light lines along his head.

Teddy started to bark and cautiously inch in closer. It did not take the snake long to feel threatened. He struck fast and hard on Teddy's front leg and slithered away. Teddy howled in pain, and the world in the swamp stopped for a moment. Buck and Lady ran back to the area and saw Teddy sinking down to the ground and crying. No one was sure what happened; all they knew was that Teddy was in trouble. He lay trembling and whining. Buck and Lady looked him over, licked his face, and sat down to figure out what to do.

The snake's venom was very toxic; this type of snake is considered one of the most dangerous in America. Bites from them are very serious and potentially deadly.

The three dogs lay together for a while. Teddy rose after a few minutes, noticing the area where he had been bitten was red and swelling. He felt nauseated. As he rose to his feet, he looked at the other dogs. Everyone got up and continued along toward the other side of the woods, headed to the store. Teddy slowly followed, holding up his front leg when possible.

It seemed to take forever, but they came to the clearing and started across the street. Buck looked back to see Teddy sinking down at the edge of the clearing. He couldn't go on and was sick and throwing up. Buck was worried about his friend but continued across the street with Lady close behind.

Buck noticed the park ranger's truck at the store. He waited patiently for him to come out, all the while glancing over at Teddy lying at the edge of the clearing across the street.

Several people came and went, and they always looked down at Buck and Lady. No one cared to linger and get acquainted, however. Buck and Lady continued to stay posted near the door.

The park ranger often stopped in to chat with local merchants. He sometimes bought nothing but just visited. When he came to the door, he immediately saw the dogs. He came out and said, "Well, well, well, you are the dogs I saw this morning in the campground." Buck sat up and began whining and walking toward the street. The ranger kept observing and thought, *How strange ... wonder what he wants.* He noticed from the close-up view that Buck had problems—something going on with bloody spots on his back. He reached down to pet Lady, who calmly sat, looking adorable. Buck continued to whine and move to the street. When the ranger looked this time, he ran across the street to where Teddy was, sat down, and starting barking. The ranger said, "Oh, so that is where your little black-and-white buddy is."

A more careful look in that direction confirmed that something was wrong with the dog. He walked across the street and up to the dog lying on the ground. First he thought maybe he had been hit by a car or truck. Then he noticed the front of his leg was swollen and had blood blisters on it. Teddy was now trembling, having what appeared to be a seizure. The ranger knew immediately that it was a snakebite—a venomous snakebite.

Both dogs seemed friendly, so he went back to his truck, took out a blanket, and brought it over to the dogs. He wrapped Teddy in the blanket and moved toward the truck. He looked back at Buck and said, "Buddy, he has to get some help from the doc; do you want to go?" Buck hopped up and indicated that he was on his way. He jumped into the back of the truck and sat down while the ranger laid Teddy in the front seat. Then Buck realized that Lady was looking up at the bed of the truck, whining, unable to jump. Buck jumped out and barked at the ranger and then ran to the back of the truck. The ranger turned around, picked up Lady, and put her in the truck, and off they went to the veterinarian.

Buck had ridden in the back of a pickup truck before and loved the wind in his face as they rode along. Lady, however, had never experienced anything like this and was terrified. She lay huddled in the front corner of the truck with her pads holding like suction cups to the floor. She felt, moreover, that since she was with Buck and he showed no concern, everything would be okay. Teddy lay on the front seat, trembling and still. Every now and then, the ranger would put his hand over on Teddy's blanket to reassure him that everything was going to be okay.

Doc Sanders worked out of his house. He had started as a large-animal veterinarian, but as the community had grown, he had extended his medical services to all animals, large and small. As the ranger pulled into the driveway with the animals, Doc was getting the mail. He said, "Herby, what have you got for me today?"

Herb looked concerned and told Dock about Teddy's snakebite. He explained that the dogs appeared to be homeless and that he had seen them this morning in the campground. He glanced into the back of the pickup and said, "Those are his buddies."

Doc said, "Let's take care of the snakebite now; do you think the other two will stay in the truck?"

Herb said, "Stay put, guys; we'll be back."

They took Teddy into the medical area of the house and left Buck and Lady outside. Buck immediately jumped out of the truck when the men went inside. He coaxed Lady to jump as well. She took a tumble in the grassy driveway and made it out okay. They both went and sat on the front porch, waiting for Teddy.

While Doc Sanders put an IV into Teddy's leg and cleansed his wound, he and Herb talked about the dogs. Doc told him this was just the beginning of a huge concern for homeless animals after the hurricane. He was sympathetic but did not have an answer to the problem. What he could do, however, was try to save Teddy. He gave him a shot to counter the toxin from the snake and put him in a small cage with a towel.

Doc Sanders told Herb that Teddy would most likely be okay in a few days but needed to stay quiet until he got better. They discussed the three dogs and agreed that the first thing they should do was feed and water them. When Doc and Herb came to the door with food and water, Buck looked at Herb as though food and water were not the main concern right now. Herb told him Teddy would be fine but had to stay with Doc Sanders for a few days. Buck ate and drank alongside Lady, all the while thinking about Teddy's problem. Herb felt that the dog understood.

Doc said Herb should take the other two over to the kennel and see if Miss Kitty would take them in for adoption. Doc then saw the buckshot wounds on Buck's back and legs. He said, "Bring that one in; he looks like he's been shot. Herb held Buck by his flea collar and coaxed him into the medical facility, leaving Lady to sit on the porch and finish eating."

Doc said he had indeed been shot within the last forty-eight hours but that the wounds were already healing. He took an x-ray picture of Buck's back and legs to see if the buckshot had damaged any major organs. The dog appeared healthy otherwise. He decided to leave the buckshot alone, clean the wounds, and give Buck an antibiotic. Buck didn't care for the shot, but he knew these men were not trying to hurt him. They all went back to the porch, where Lady was waiting. Buck had been able to see Teddy in the cage, asleep. He followed Herb to the door with a wagging tail.

Herb thanked Doc for helping, picked up Lady, put her in the truck, and then patted the truck for Buck to jump up. He was going to see if Miss Kitty would be generous enough to hold the animals, thinking maybe they belonged to someone in the community.

Herb started the truck while Buck and Lady looked at each other. They exchanged some type of communication, because before the truck had moved out of the driveway, both of them had jumped out and run to the nearest forest edge. When they were far enough into the brush to feel safe, Buck stopped for Lady to catch up and rest. They both knew Teddy would be well taken care of. They had to move on. It was at least five minutes before Herb realized he had no dogs in his truck. He pulled over to the side of the road, thought about it for a minute, smiled, and then moved on. He hoped they would be okay, but he respected their wishes not to go to Miss Kitty's. This was all in a day's work for the park ranger.

Sore Pads and Thievery in Saucier

Buck decided to follow the road, staying in the brush alongside it. He and Lady trotted along, stopping from time to time to rest and drink a little water here and there.

They passed through cotton fields; it was easier walking through the dirt than through the brush. A problem was the sticky burrs that attached themselves to their fur—especially Lady's. She had started out looking like a beautiful pedigreed dog, but now her fur was gnarled with knots and burrs, and she was filthy. She was still a lady, however. She played the part to get Buck's attention when she needed it.

Once when they stopped, she began licking her paws. Buck noticed they were bruised and red. He had big, thick black pads that were tough enough to walk long distances. His cuts were healing also. But Lady was a little Fifi-type of dog who sat on pillows looking pretty. Buck had created a close bond with Lady and was considerate to her in every way possible. The sun was going down, so soon they would stop for the night. Buck wasn't sure where he was going, but he seemed to have a purpose.

They stopped soon thereafter at a pond with weeping willow trees overhanging the water. It was part of a farm but was far enough away from the house to be safe from irate farmers. Both Buck and Lady lay full-out in the shade near the water to rest. Buck fell into a deep sleep for the first time since he was home with Ben in his bed. He snored and enjoyed the cool ground. Lady was totally exhausted and lay with her paws touching the edge of the water; it was soothing to her sore pads. They slept till dark.

After napping, Buck woke to darkness and Lady licking her paws. He went over to her and helped her lick out the soreness. Her paws tasted like the water in the pond. She was enjoying the attention and watching a bullfrog nearby blowing out his croaking throat and making a strange sound she had never heard before. Buck looked up and poised himself for a frog leap. When he started moving, the frog jumped into the pond. It felt good to have fun again—just like when he and Ben went fishing.

Buck left Lady for a while to hunt the area. He stalked through the brush, looking for movement. He saw a rabbit sitting quietly ahead, munching on fresh, succulent grass. He stopped, went into a point position, and began walking stealthily, moving three steps at a time and then stopping. He was surprised how close he was getting without the rabbit noticing. He was really absorbed in his dinner.

He came within two feet of the rabbit and took off in a dead run. The rabbit was fast, but Buck was close and smelled the kill. He ran the rabbit through the field about a quarter mile and then was able to grab him with his powerful jaws. He held on for dear life all the while the rabbit was kicking and floundering around. The rabbit suddenly went limp, and Buck felt as if he had won the Kentucky Derby. He had never caught a rabbit before and felt very accomplished. He picked up the rabbit in his mouth and headed back to the pond to share dinner with Lady.

Buck laid the rabbit in front of Lady and began to tear away the skin. He wasn't starved, as he had eaten that morning, but the smell of blood and fresh game excited him. He dived in, eating what he wanted. He looked up at Lady, who was watching the whole incident with horror. She would starve to death before she ate raw meat from a fresh kill. It just wasn't part of her makeup. Buck somehow understood and finished off what he wanted. He went to the pond to drink and ended up wading around in the water. He felt good. He could see fish, and it had always fascinated him to watch them. At least his little hike in the water cleaned off most of the rabbit's blood from his body.

Buck and Lady lay together by a tree in a soft pad of grass, just enjoying the night and the comfort of their area. The frogs continued to croak into the night; locusts sang their song by rubbing their legs together, and the night was beautiful.

The next morning, Buck and Lady got an early start, walking close, but not too close, to the road. Along the way, they passed houses, and they always surveyed with caution to see whether there was an opportunity for food. They stopped numerous times to rest and once took a short nap. Several hours later, they saw a city just ahead on the road—Saucier.

From the Doc's house in Lyman the previous day, they traveled about nine miles to Saucier, Mississippi. Saucier, like Lyman, was a small community with a population of around thirteen hundred. The town was mostly made up of farmers and construction workers. Mississippi, on the average, has half its people living below the poverty line.

Buck and Lady came upon a lumber distribution center for the construction business in town. The smell of freshly cut wood was familiar to Buck's nose. He was drawn to the site. It was end of the workday, and he could see men coming to and going from the site just like he remembered at home.

The dogs wandered into the main entrance, headed toward the office building and loading dock. Lady almost got hit by a truck that was leaving by not staying close enough to Buck. She scurried up to his rear and remained frightened. Buck sat down near an office door, and Lady followed suit.

Buck carefully watched each person leaving the building, with the thought that just maybe Jake was here. Buck waited for over an hour till all the employees had left the building. Jake had not come out. He glanced back at Lady, who was licking some snack wrappers at the end of the building. Food, especially for Lady, replaced his thoughts of waiting, so he left his post and walked toward town with Lady following.

He saw a grocery store and headed in that direction. After sitting at the door for nearly an hour, only a few people had looked in their direction. Buck looked at Lady as if to tell her to stay. He slipped in through the front door and stealthily crept behind food displays as he circled the store. Behind a huge fall display of pumpkins, he eyed the meat stacked in the coolers. He lunged toward the deli and grabbed a rotisserie chicken package and made like a bandit to the door. He didn't have to say anything to Lady. When she saw him racing out of the store and down the street, she scurried behind him.

Someone in the store had seen Buck run up to the counter and went to get a store employee. By that time, Buck was gone. The people were baffled that a dog had gotten into the store unseen and had stolen meat without much resistance. Buck had just become a thief—all in the name of survival. He had to get food for Lady; she wouldn't eat his hunted game.

They ran into an alley behind a commercial strip of shops and found a secluded corner where they could devour their food. Lady ate slowly but well. Lady's mouth was small, and her little nibbles were nothing compared to Buck's big mouth and sharp white teeth. In less than half an hour, every piece of the chicken was gone, except for a couple of drumstick bones. The dogs each took a bone and headed on to a grassy area to sit and gnaw on their savory catch.

By now word had spread to a few shops that a wild dog was on the loose, stealing food. It concerned some people, as the dog could be rabid and dangerous. The grocery store called animal control and was promised that they would search the area. Animal control was nothing more than a volunteer-operated city-sponsored program with a small facility and two employees. The manager got into his truck and started down the street, searching for a wild dog. He had a pretty good description of Buck.

The animal control manager perused all the streets and alleys, looking for the dog. Just about when he was ready to give up, he spotted two dogs sitting close to an alley, chewing on bones. He jumped out of the truck with his net and tried to creep up closer to their location. Buck noticed the guy and got up. Lady continued to gnaw her bone. Buck barked. Lady sat up and noticed, alarmed, and they both started running.

It was no problem for Buck to outrun the man, but Lady was much slower; she was netted. Buck stood back and watched the man put her in the truck and secure the lock. The man came back to chase Buck, but Buck retreated out of sight and far ahead of the man. The man turned back to the truck. Buck crept behind him.

The man drove off with Lady, and Buck followed the truck, trying to stay out of sight. They went to the animal control center, and the man unloaded poor Lady and threw her into a cage. He began to recount his experiences to his colleague and phoned the market to let them know he had caught one of the dogs.

Buck hid close by, observing what happened with Lady. He heard the guy say he had to continue his search for the other dog. He then got back into the truck and drove away. His colleague looked at the dog in the cage and then went back to the building to continue reading his book.

Lady lay down, looking totally forlorn. She had been confined before for short periods, but not like this. There were two dogs in other cages, barking. The guy came out of the building and turned a hose of water on the barking dogs; they quieted down.

Late that night, when it seemed all personnel were gone, Buck visited Lady and observed that she was locked away and he was unable to free her. During the night, he lay for a while touching her cage with her close on the other side of the fence. The other three dogs seemed to understand his presence and did not make noise.

Before morning, Buck hid in some nearby bushes and stayed close by. Around 9:00 a.m., one of the men came around to start his daily work. He hosed out the cages and filled the dogs' water bowls. He hosed the dogs to keep the smell down. He left for a while and came back with a bag of food. He went to the far end, starting with the dogs that had already been there when Lady arrived, and squeezed into their cages to pour some dry food on the floor. The dogs ate heartily. When he reached Lady's cage, Buck ran from his post, knocked down the man with the bag of food, and gave Lady a chance to get out. He and Lady ran like bandits into a new day.

They ran for at least a mile before stopping outside town in a cornfield. They cooled their heels in the field, which gave them good cover. Lady licked Buck all over his face; she was so glad to see him. Her damp fur from the hosing was beginning to dry, but what a tangled mess she was.

Buck knew they had to get out of town and eventually began walking again close to the road—but not too close.

Wilma Witherspoon in McHenry, Mississippi

Buck and Lady had begun to tire of the road trip. Buck's search for something that would lead him home or to his family was very frustrating and disappointing. Lady wasn't sure where they were going, but knew she felt safer with Buck. This certainly proved to be true, as he had rescued her more than once. She felt a deep affection for Buck.

Today's hike was not as long—only about five miles. Lady's paws were still bruised and swollen. Buck tried to keep them in the grass, which was much less abusive to her feet than the pavement—not to mention the heat. Both of them trudged along with their tongues hanging out.

They happened upon what appeared to be a small farm. The house was on the outskirts of McHenry, Mississippi-a beautiful Victorian home that looked inviting. It was the home of the late Dr. G. A. McHenry, who had received recognition from the historical society in 1934 for the fine architecture of his home. After all these years, it still looked like a picture in a book.

As Buck and Lady approached, they heard some unfamiliar singing from the back of the house. It happened that the cook was a Chinese man by the name of Wong On. Wong was cooking supper for Mrs. Wilma Witherspoon, who owned the house. Many years ago, she had acquired a taste for Chinese cooking and had convinced Wong to come to work for her when he closed his restaurant in McHenry. Wong and his wife, Kit-Mui, were offered an apartment in the big house and care from Ms. Witherspoon for as long as the arrangement worked.

Tonight Kit and Wong were preparing barbequed chicken, fresh stir-fried vegetables—including Wong's favorite, bok choy—and fresh melon. Kit grew most of the vegetables they cooked in a beautiful Chinese garden near the house.

Kit's singing and Wong's clatter of pots and pans were happy sounds to Buck and Lady. They continued to approach the back of the house, smelling the aromas from the kitchen. They sat near the back door, hoping for a positive response to their presence.

Kit looked out the screen door and screamed something in Chinese in a high-pitched voice and danced around until Wong came. When Wong heard her scream, he dropped his pan, which made him angry along with his concern for Kit's scream. He started ranting and raving as he approached the door, where Kit stood with her hands over her mouth looking as if she had seen a ghost.

When the singing and cooking changed to swearing and screaming, Buck and Lady began to move away from the door. Buck was looking over his shoulder in a bewildered way while he led Lady back. Lady had her head down, looking pitiful.

Wong put his arm around Kit, gazed out the door and said, "Ah, ah," in a long, drawn-out understanding tone. Kit had tears in her eyes, and Wong hugged her closer. Wong talked softly to Kit for a minute, and then they both opened the door and started sweetly begging the dogs to come.

This was very confusing for the dogs, and Buck wasn't sure he should trust these unpredictable, strange people. Buck and Lady remained stopped in their tracks and just looked at Wong and Kit.

Wong turned and went into the house. He came out with a bowl of chicken tidbits. It was all they needed; the dogs slowly approached the bowl.

All the while, Kit was still crying and sweetly talking, directing most of her body language toward Lady. As the dogs approached the bowl, she smiled and waited for them to eat. She baby-talked to the dogs and slowly stooped to stroke Lady. When she was able to touch Lady, she uttered soothing words and asked Wong if she could pick her up.

Wong looked at Buck, who could have a somewhat threatening look if he wanted to, and told Kit to take it slowly; perhaps sit down and take a little time to get acquainted so she wouldn't bolt and run.

What was happening here was that Wong and Kit had kept a female Pekinese for eighteen years after they came to Mississippi. She had been the center of their lives all through the days when they were first tenant farmers, then owners of a grocery store, and finally the owners of a restaurant. It had been six years since their baby girl died, and Kit had never let go of the daily grieving.

Kit and Wong never had children, so their pet, Ming, was a major part of the family. They would not have been able to be as openly loving of a dog in China; therefore, they had felt blessed every day with Ming.

Kit felt that the gods had sent this angel to her in answer to all her prayers and repentance of her sins. The fact that Lady's appearance since she had been on the run was nothing like it had been mattered not to Kit. Lady's matted, dirty fur could once again be a beautiful silky coat. She would spend all her spare time tediously working through the knots in her coat to restore her beauty.

Wong broke the silence by noting that they had to speak with Mrs. Witherspoon about the dog. After all, a dog had not been part of the agreement they made when they came to work for her. He turned and went back into the kitchen to clean up his mess and continue with dinner. Kit was entranced, loving on Lady, and Lady was in heaven from the attention and the touch of a loving human hand.

Buck sat off to the side, watching the whole thing transpire. He felt left out and wasn't sure what to do next. He went over and lay down in the shade of a large tree to continue his observations.

Wong came out of the house with Mrs. Witherspoon. Wong took a long time to tell her the whole story—one which she was not aware of. She stood looking at Kit, Lady, and Buck and listening to Wong. There was a long pause when no one said anything but just looked at the dogs, and the dogs looked at them. Mrs. Witherspoon finally broke the silence and said, "First things first, we need to see if these two belong to someone in the area; there are dogs coming through from the south every day; I imagine they are homeless now, having run from the hurricane. The pound is picking up dogs every day, so let's put them into the shed until we know more."

Kit picked up Lady as if she were a china doll and held her to her breast while walking toward the shed. Mrs. Witherspoon and Wong followed to make a place for the dogs to sleep. They went into the shed and began moving things around to open up an area for the dogs. Wong filled up a bowl with fresh water and placed it near the window. Kit ran back to the house and returned with a soft towel to use as a bed. Lady immediately lay on the towel, happy to be on something soft. Lady seemed to know that everything was going to be all right.

Wong came to the door and called for Buck to come. Buck was reluctant to be closed inside a shed and stood his ground. Wong tried to approach Buck, who steadily moved away from Wong.

Mrs. Witherspoon observed what was happening and said, "He might be wild; leave him alone. He sure is a handsome dog though." So they closed the shed door and left Lady alone inside while Buck walked into the woods nearby.

Buck watched from afar until the people went into the house. He lay down in the woods and waited for something, though he wasn't sure what. He suddenly felt lonely and unsure of himself.

Kit made several more trips to the shed that night to check on Lady and finally locked the back door and went to bed. As Buck quietly crept to the shed and lay down outside the door, Mrs. Witherspoon was watching from her bedroom window. She wondered about the dogs, and many memories passed through her mind. Mrs. Witherspoon was a storyteller, so the unknown was of much interest to her. She was an avid Mississippi historian, and anything that raised a question made her head spin with possibilities. One thing was for sure: there was a bond between the two dogs, however unlikely it seemed. The larger dog almost seemed protective of the little one. She would play the waiting game and keep her eyes and ears open to queries about lost dogs.

Mrs. Witherspoon's husband, John—God rest his soul—had been a dog lover. It was eerie that the big dog looked much like her husband's beloved Australian cattle dog. John had been so proud of his "Hoss," as he called him. The breed was a bit unusual, and lots of attention was always bestowed on John and Hoss when they were out in the community. Hoss had died shortly after John's death. Mrs. Witherspoon had always wondered if Hoss had died of grief for John.

She turned out the light and gave one more tug at the curtain to see the dog curled up in front of the door of the shed. She went to bed thinking that maybe these animals had been sent to her and Kit. She always believed that if one was a good person and filling his or her life with kindness to others and the love of God, good things would come to him or her.

During the night, the two dogs sniffed each other through the crack in the door. Lady was a little confused about the separation and stood up at the door, scratching and whining. When Buck lay back down where she could see that he was near, she went back to her bed.

Buck felt loyalty to their friendship and wanted to remain with Lady. He had some anxiety, however, about what was going to happen next. Lady was very attached to Buck and didn't understand what to do, but she felt calm about the people they had met. She loved the way Kit touched her and held her close. It was something she had missed since her family left.

Bonding with Buck

Kit rose at dawn and rushed outside to check on Lady. Buck was surprised by her early arrival and ran around to the back of the shed to avoid her. She barely noticed Buck; all that was on her mind was getting inside the shed to see her angel. Lady was happy to see Kit and rose from the soft towel to greet her.

Kit brought out a napkin filled with yummy leftovers from last night's dinner. She had a wet washcloth and washed Lady's face after she ate, paying close attention to her eyes, where tears had run down and left a dark path. She would bathe Lady today and work on her matted coat. After spending as long as she could loving and talking to Lady, she left and closed the shed door.

Buck could smell the food and hear the soft, soothing voice of Kit. After she left, he decided to resume his post at the door, with a watchful eye on the kitchen door.

At breakfast Mrs. Witherspoon asked Kit about the dogs. As Kit was serving breakfast, she told her about her early-morning visit to the shed. She asked Kit about the bigger dog, and Kit mumbled something about the dog running away.

Mrs. Witherspoon finished her breakfast and went to the back to look outside. The larger dog was still posted outside the shed door. She turned around and called Wong and Kit into the dining room. Kit was terrified that Mrs. Witherspoon had decided they could not keep the little angel.

Mrs. Witherspoon looked carefully at the couple as they stood in front of her. She told them to sit down with a cup of tea. After a few minutes, everyone was settled at the table, Wong and Kit looking a bit nervous.

Wong and Kit had come to work for her about two years before her husband, John, had died. Her former housekeeper/cook was getting too old to do the job and decided to move back to Alabama to be with her family.

Mrs. Witherspoon asked them if they remembered Hoss. Both nodded anxiously and then shook their heads, referring to his death. She asked if they thought the larger dog resembled Hoss. They paused and then, surprising themselves, agreed. They weren't sure where this conversation was going.

Wong spoke with reverence about John Witherspoon and what a fine man he was. Mrs. Witherspoon nodded. She added that one of his most valuable assets, according to John, was Hoss, and that he had adored the ground the dog had walked on. Both Wong and Kit nodded.

Mrs. Witherspoon then announced that there seemed to be a reason these dogs had come to them; she suggested that perhaps God had led them there, and that perhaps it was meant that these dogs become part of their family. After all, Mrs. Witherspoon, with her failing health, could use some happy moments. She had an agenda to do God's will. She felt her last years should be spent passing on as much information to her grandchildren about their heritage and their family as possible so as not to lose the connection—the important link to their past, with their ancestors being some of Mississippi's great leaders. Perhaps the dogs were part of this journey to fill the gaps with as much joy as possible. After all, didn't they feel the little dog had been a blessing sent to them for a reason? How coincidental that the little dog was exactly the same breed and gender as their former pet. And how coincidental that the larger dog looked very much like Hoss. This strengthened her memories of John and his loving spirit. It gave her comfort.

Both Wong and Kit smiled broadly and jumped from their seats to hug Mrs. Witherspoon. When the celebratory gestures were over, she asked Wong if Hoss had been fed. He looked at Kit and she relayed her morning's activities. They were about to run from the kitchen when Mrs. Witherspoon said, "We have to bond with this dog to get his trust; he and the smaller dog are emotionally attached, and it would not be good to separate them." Wong and Kit ran to the kitchen to make a big bowl of breakfast for Buck.

Mrs. Witherspoon followed and said she wanted to give Hoss his bowl. She cautiously and slowly left the house and stopped outside the door. She looked at Buck and showed him the bowl. She told him in a calm voice that it was for him. She walked over to the swing in the yard and put the bowl a few feet away and began coaxing him to come. He had alerted to her appearance and looked surprised and unsure of what to do. He had no reason to think these people would harm him, so he came up to the bowl and wolfed down the meal. He looked up at Mrs. Witherspoon as if to say thanks as he licked his chops, and she smiled. He went back to the shed and lay down. Mrs. Witherspoon told Wong to replace the bowl with a big bowl of water for him. Mrs. Witherspoon felt that if they eventually moved into the shed with his meals, he would follow.

The days went by, repeating themselves, with meals being given to the dogs and Buck's bowl moving closer and closer to the inside of the shed. No one attempted to chase him or scare him in any way. On the fifth day, success was achieved with Buck going into the shed to eat. Mrs. Witherspoon and Kit stayed inside with the dogs. Kit continued her loving gestures toward Lady, and Mrs. Witherspoon sat quietly near the door, talking every now and then to Buck, telling him how special he was. Buck moved to her chair, and Mrs. Witherspoon began to pet him, stroking his fur and rubbing his velvety ears. All the while, tears were pouring down her face. She stayed for at least an hour, paying all her attention to Buck. She then looked at Kit and said, "I think we can leave the shed door cracked or open now. Get Wong to bring out a blanket."

Mrs. Witherspoon's Agenda

Another week had passed with progress being made regarding the bonding of the people and the dogs. Both dogs had baths, and hours were spent brushing and untangling Lady's fur coat. Lady came inside the house immediately after her bath and made herself at home on a soft chair. More attention was given to Buck's wounds, each one touched with a Q-tip covered in bacterial salve.

Both the dogs acquired new names to fit the fond memories of former pets: "Hoss" and "Angel".

Mrs. Witherspoon called Dr. Hendrix to come out to the house and give both dogs a physical examination. He and Mrs. Witherspoon discussed Hoss's gunshot wounds. They were crusting over and healing now; but the doctor said the pellets would need to stay and probably wouldn't cause him any serious problems. When she learned what they were, Mrs. Witherspoon teared up with sympathy and respect for Hoss. No one knew what these two dogs had gone through to get there.

With coaxing, Hoss began to come into the house fairly often. He loved to lie on the cool wooden floor as well as the far end of the sofa. He would curl up on the sofa and put his head up on the arm of the sofa so he could see what was going on. He almost always seemed to be on guard.

Occasionally he would take a deep sleep and snore. Mrs. Witherspoon would giggle and feel compelled to stroke his long, velvety black nose. Sometimes she would sit beside Hoss on the sofa for hours, amusing herself with him. Both Hoss and Angel picked up quickly on their new names, especially since their use usually meant food or love was coming.

Mrs. Witherspoon's grandchildren were coming over one weekend, and they couldn't wait to meet the new pets. It was a big surprise to the family that Mrs. Witherspoon had worked so hard to keep these two dogs. They knew they pair must be something special. It was a happy thought that the pets were giving Mrs. Witherspoon such joy. She had been quietly depressed since the death of John, and her health seemed to be sliding in a downward spiral every time they saw her.

The grandchildren, Douglas and Tiffany, ages eleven and nine, always looked forward to a special story from Grandma Witherspoon. She always prepared one for them, and all the time after dinner until bedtime was devoted to everyone in the living room listening to the story. It was rare for them to not make it through the entire story and fall asleep, but it had happened at times. There was usually lively discussion of the story afterward over dessert.

Angel was all prettied up, with her blonde coat of long, flowing, silky fur brushed with every hair in place. Kit had pulled up the fur on top of her head and secured it with a ribbon. She had a little sprig of hair on top of her head that bounced around when she turned her pretty head. Angel knew she was beautiful and batted her eyes to show off.

Hoss was clean, comfortable, and well fed. That was really all he cared about. While he was not fond of being brushed, he tolerated it pretty well. He was really handsome, with a shiny, thick coat of fur. His tail was as bushy as a raccoon's; it was one of the more unique things about him. His face had a sharp black nose, big, expressive eyes, and large pointed ears. It was good that he allowed the brushing, because he had an undercoat that needed to be brushed out in this hot weather. Hoss's colors looked like those of a Bundt cake—dark chocolate with lots of caramel swirls all over.

Wong and Kit were busy cleaning the house, changing the beds, dusting, and, of course, cooking all the kids' favorite foods. Family was always a celebration at the house, and happiness filled every room. Fresh flowers were cut from the garden and displayed in all rooms. Extra care was taken to dust and clean all the family pictures. The good china and silverware were always used. It gave Wong and Kit special honor that this weekend they would be using the Chinese china pattern that had been handed down over the years to Mrs. Witherspoon's family from the McHenrys.

Mrs. Witherspoon planned to surprise Wong and Kit and tell the children about the Mississippi Chinese who came after the Civil War. She always regarded Wong and Kit as family, even though in some circles—especially in the South—the "help" kept to themselves.

On Saturday, Charles and Amanda McHenry-Witherspoon drove into the driveway with the children spilling out of the car and running toward the house. The children brought Grandma her favorite chocolates. Wong and Kit were given hugs and a box of fall bulbs to be planted in the garden for spring. Charles and Amanda even had doggie treats in their pockets for the new arrivals. It was a party with lots of smiles, hugs, kisses, and joy.

Charles managed his mother's cotton production. The plantation's cotton had been a source of income handled down in the family since the early 1900s.

After the splendid dinner, everyone gathered in the living room. Wong and Kit prepared the coffee table with luscious tea, both hot and iced. The children had never acquired a taste for hot tea.

Charles and Hoss had made fast friends. Hoss took his normal place at the end of the sofa, with Charles sitting on the floor in front of the sofa to be near Hoss. Tiffany thought Angel was the most precious thing she had ever seen. She was like a princess sitting on her chair. Tiffany squeezed into the chair with Angel, and together the two girls settled in for a story.

Charles and Amanda were beaming as they watched the children, who were so taken with the dogs. Mrs. Witherspoon was especially happy that the dogs had been well behaved and allowed the children to enjoy them so much. With all in their places with full stomachs and love in their hearts, Mrs. Witherspoon started her story.

Mississippi Chinese

A small group of Chinese immigrants came to Mississippi after the Civil War. In their new surroundings, they looked for ways to earn money and to adapt to the culture of the state while still preserving their own ethnic identity. Mississippi had a dominance of British and African ancestry.

Their arrival occurred during a time of considerable turmoil in Mississippi as the state adjusted after the Civil War to the end of slavery and the defeat of the Confederacy. This was called the Reconstruction period and was around 1865. This period lasted for twelve years.

Tensions were high between the black freedmen and the whites. Because the labor system was unsettled, planters recruited the Chinese as possible replacements for the freed African American laborers. The US census in 1880 listed fifty-one Chinese in Mississippi.

Most Chinese immigrants coming to Mississippi were mainly from the Sze Yap, an area in south China. Sze Yap was a more advanced and sophisticated area of China at the time, with a history of contacts with foreign traders. Immigrants were most likely from peasant and artisan families. Traditionally, young males from the area traveled far for work to supplement the family income. Initially the immigrants who came to

Mississippi came only to earn money to send back home or save for the time when they would return to China. After the original fifty-one, more and more immigrants came—mostly men; the few women who came remained socially isolated. The Chinese were classified as nonwhite in a biracial Mississippi social system. Some Chinese married blacks as time went by.

The Chinese were looking for economic success. However, they soon realized that working on a plantation did not produce economic success. Many Chinese turned to another activity—opening and running grocery stores. The grocery stores in this period were small one-room shacks that carried a few basics, such as meat, cornmeal, and molasses. The people who shopped at the stores were mostly poor blacks working on plantations or laborers working to drain the swamps and cut timber in the delta.

In those days, there were no self-service stores; customers had to ask for what they wanted. Merely buying a sack of cornmeal was a complicated matter; the Chinese shop owners at first did not speak English, and their customers did not know Chinese. There was a lot of pointing at the merchandise. Sometimes other businessmen took advantage of the Chinese because of their lack of understanding of the English language. The Chinese were somewhat vulnerable in the southern legal system.

Chinese grocers, nonetheless, carved out a successful and distinctive role. One reason for their success was a cohesive family system. After they established their small businesses, these early Chinese merchants would send back home for a young male from their family to come and help the business succeed and to learn how to run a business. That young relative would later perhaps use his savings, loans from relatives, and credit from wholesale suppliers to set up his own grocery. Hard work, experience in business operations, and a reputation for financial integrity soon led to good credit ratings for the Chinese merchants. For generations, grocery stores would be passed down from father to son, and as late as the 1970s, six family names accounted for 80 percent of the delta Chinese population.

The Chinese became middlemen between blacks and whites, often providing a needed contact point in a segregated society. Even though white Mississippians originally classified the Chinese in the delta on a low social par with African Americans, blacks and whites did not, however, see Chinese as equivalent to blacks. Their merchant status was above that of most blacks.

Chinese in the delta attempted to maintain a certain distance from others in society, hoping to insulate themselves from problems and concentrate on their economic status. They were excluded from social organizations, country clubs, recreational activities, and, most importantly, white public schools. Several delta cities had separate schools for whites, blacks, and Chinese. Additionally, Chinese cemeteries were separate—typically small, well-tended plots with high fences around them.

The Chinese worked over the years to affiliate with the white community as much as possible because whites held the highest social status. Naming patterns came to reflect this change. Chinese parents might pick first names of their children like "Coleman" and "Patricia" to suggest identification with whites.

The tong was a social organization that structured much delta Chinese social activity in the early days. But by the 1930s, the Baptist Church became important for the Chinese and served as a center for wedding banquets, funerals, community activities, and other occasions. The mission school attached to the church provided education for the Chinese, preparing them for identification with white society.

Since the 1960s, the Chinese in Mississippi have faced the decline of their economic base as distinctive delta grocers serving a black clientele. Blacks now have more choices of grocery stores, including large chain stores. Children of Chinese families go away to school now and often do not seek to inherit and run old businesses. Many Chinese have moved to nearby mid-south cities, such as Jackson and Memphis. The Chinese who remain, and newcomers who still arrive seeking economic opportunity, run Chinese restaurants. Families celebrate traditional Chinese holidays, out of sight of most Mississippians, to honor their ancestors.

The delta was settled by other ethnic groups as well as the Chinese. Lebanese, Syrians, Jews, Mexicans, and Italians all play notable roles there, but the Chinese had perhaps the most challenging adjustment because they came from a culture that seemed unusual to most other Mississippians.

Even though the Chinese were small in number, they filled a distinctive economic role as merchants; they won the friendship of the African Americans and the whites, who came to trust their honesty in business dealings. Still, the Chinese made new lives as southerners and became a notable feature of delta society. The 2000 census reported that over three thousand Chinese lived in Mississippi, out of an Asian population of over eighteen thousand in the state.

It was then that Mrs. Witherspoon honored the presence of Wong and Kit in the family and expressed appreciation for their contributions. Both Wong and Kit were glued to every word that had been said, as they had relived a lot of this history in their own world. They now felt blessed to be part of the Witherspoon household.

The family asked a lot of questions of Wong and Kit, now having a better understanding of their lives in Mississippi. Wong and Kit graciously answered each one until the children began to nod. Kit went to turn down their beds. The children followed, sleepy-eyed.

Douglas put on his pajamas and crawled up into the high bed to snuggle under the soft sheets. He looked down and saw Hoss sitting by the bed, looking at him with begging brown eyes. Douglas said, "Come on, boy." Hoss jumped on the bed immediately and curled up next to Douglas. Douglas draped his arm across Hoss, and they both fell fast asleep.

It is a good thing that Tiffany slept in the room with her parents in the trundle bed and was not able to notice that Douglas was sleeping with Hoss. She would have been disappointed that she didn't have a dog to sleep with.

Angel, when the children stirred from their chairs in the living room, got up and immediately disappeared to Wong and Kit's room, where she slept at the foot of their bed.

Mrs. Witherspoon had another cup of tea while everyone got settled. She then got up to make her way back to her bedroom. She was very tired tonight and couldn't wait to get to bed. She thanked Wong and Kit on her way back. She peeked in on Douglas and saw Hoss snuggled as close as possible to Douglas with his head on the pillow. Her heart sang with joy, and she smiled broadly. As Charles was coming out of the bathroom to cross the hall, she motioned for him to come look. They stood together with arms intertwined, taking in the heartwarming sight. Charles went in to kiss Douglas's forehead, and Mrs. Witherspoon went to bed.

Grandma, Please, One More Story

The next day was filled with fun, good food, and interesting activities. Kit took the children to the garden and let them help her pick squash, zucchini, tomatoes, and peppers for the evening meal. Hoss stayed with Douglas all day. Angel took time out between naps to let Amanda hold her, brush her, and love her. Charles and Amanda spent time with Grandma. During each visit, they had serious business conversations about the cotton crop each year, as this was Charles's main concern for the family. Lately they had been concerned about Grandma's declining health and wanted to make sure they took care of everything Grandma needed.

After lunch, the children begged Grandma for one more story before they had to leave. Grandma looked tired but consented to find some light material to share with them. She promised to keep it as short as possible but didn't want to leave out anything. After all, she had a fair number of stories left on her agenda for the children and wanted to make sure she got them all in before she was no longer able.

"Just over one hundred years ago," Grandma said, "many homes in Mississippi and other rural American states did not have indoor plumbing or adequate sanitary facilities." "Families could rarely afford to install indoor plumbing. Also, many Mississippians did not know how to properly dispose of waste and prevent disease." "As a result, they were often plagued with diseases that were directly linked to unsanitary facilities." "Hookworm was one such disease."

"For hookworms to survive, they must live only in sandy or loamy soil—just like the soil found in the Mississippi region." "Also, to survive, hookworms must have rainfall averages of more than forty inches a year and a temperature over fifty degrees." "If these conditions exist, then the hookworm eggs hatch." "After hatching, the larvae undergo two molts and transform into threadlike worms about one half of an inch long." "They can then infect unsuspecting humans by boring into their bare feet, or occasionally their hands, as the victim walks or works around the infested soil."

"Doctors believe the slaves from Africa carried the hookworms in their intestines and introduced them to the United States."

"The life cycle of the hookworm begins and ends in the human intestinal tract." Females may lay from five thousand to twenty thousand eggs a day after mating with the male in the intestines." "The eggs are then discharged in bowel movements." "So you see, hookworm eggs constantly enter the soil in very large numbers."

"When the larvae contact the human foot or hand and bore into the skin, a rash at the site of entry erupts and itches. Back when hookworm infections were common, this was called 'ground itch' or 'dew itch,' because the larvae are most active when dew is on the ground and temperatures are warm."

"Many southerners did not wear shoes in summer months, and the larvae usually penetrated between people's toes." "In about a week, the larvae would have made it to the small intestine." "The larvae have a pair of curved cutting plates in their mouths that allow them to attach to a person's intestinal walls." "They live there, sucking the victim's blood, for about four to five years."

"People infected with hookworms often experienced a lack of energy, coughing, wheezing, and sometimes fever." "They could also have stomach pains, pale yellowish-colored skin, feet that would go to sleep, head and joint aches, vomiting, constipation, and diarrhea." "Two classic signs of hookworm disease are a pot belly and 'angel's wings'—shoulder blades that extend outward because of the person's slumping, emaciated body." "Blurred vision and a fish-eye stare characterize severe cases."

"The primary danger of hookworm disease is anemia, because the worms live on a person's plasma and excrete the red blood cells." "Death could result, depending on the number of worms in a person's gut." "Hookworms are totally dependent on humans to continue their life cycle."

"Doctors knew about hookworms, but the issue was not addressed widely until a million-dollar donation from the Rockefeller Sanitation Commission was given for the eradication of the disease." "The director of public health for Mississippi began a three-staged plan to cope with the disease—mostly around public education."

"The regions of Mississippi that were most infested because of the soil and climate conditions were Long Leaf Pine and Short Leaf Pine districts, and the coastal region." Exhibits at the state and county fairs allowed a lot of people to learn how to control the spread of the worms through proper sanitation."

"Also the schools were targeted throughout the state." "Students were tested in the most infested regions." "Instructions were sent home to parents on how to take proper health measures, such as the need to wear shoes and how to build sanitary privies, or outhouses." "Can you believe that before privies were provided in the schools, the bathroom facilities were one side of the woods for boys and the other side for girls?"

"The people in Mississippi reacted positively to these efforts and sought treatment, and they either improved their sanitary facility or constructed a new one."

"A single dose of thymol would kill the worms, and this was followed later by an enema, usually of Epsom salts, to rid the body of the dead worms." "Later tetracholorethylene became the preferred treatment."

"Even though the disease was seriously reduced starting in 1910, hookworms continued to be a health problem in Mississippi as late as the 1980s, when sixty-nine cases were reported."

"At the turn of the twenty-first century, hookworm disease was virtually unheard of in Mississippi because of education, proper sanitation, and good medical practices."

The children's eyes were very wide, and at times during the story Grandma had noticed them frowning and giving adverse looks. She knew this was not a very pleasant story, but it was an important one, as it was part of Mississippi history.

Amanda closed her notebook and put it away. She took copious notes of all Grandma's stories; she knew how valuable they were to the family. Grandma's education and work at the historical society had given them all a gift. Through the stories, Grandma was able to fulfill her passion for Mississippi history, and everyone else was able to get information that made all their lives much richer.

Charles and Amanda gathered the children and all their belongings and herded the kids toward the car. Hugs and kisses were exchanged by all. Even Hoss and Angel sat waiting for theirs. Charles took a long time hugging Hoss and talking to him. He couldn't wait to come back as soon as possible.

Mrs. Witherspoon was exhausted and told Wong and Kit she planned a long sleep.

Cozy as a Bedbug in McHenry

Thanksgiving and Christmas at Mrs. Witherspoon's was a memorable time—this year especially. Holiday dinners thoughtfully prepared by Wong and Kit were always savored and held a special place in the family's memory. Special times with the family gathered round for Grandmother's stories were memorable, not to mention the addition of Angel and Hoss to the family. Grandmother Witherspoon continued her agenda, and the grandchildren flourished through it all, not realizing how special their lives were, having been born to an elite class of people with rich history.

The winter air cooled the days and offered more dismal, rainy weather to the forecast. Some nights were cold; Hoss and Angel had no idea how good life had become for the homeless. While spending crisp, cold nights snuggled up by the fire, all the while getting all the love they could possibly hope for, Hoss and Angel snoozed through the winter, never looking back, remembering only the worst of the past.

As spring came early in Mississippi, getting to spend more time outdoors during the day pleased Hoss. He lazed in the sunshine, chased whatever crossed his path, and investigated the farm to its fullest. It was a great place to stroll through the woods, across the fields, and down the creek, sniffing all the woodsy smells. He ventured far and near on the farm, leaving his scent wherever he went. He marked the area proudly as his own and held his head high, with an attitude. He came home every evening to a full plate, a nurturing home, and a warm bed. Somehow Mrs. Witherspoon never worried that Hoss would leave; they had some sort of bond that superseded any doubt about their relationship. Mrs. Witherspoon and the family grew to love Hoss as a valuable asset in their lives. Hoss understood the silent contract he had with the Witherspoons. He was happy and content.

Angel loved spending a few minutes several times a day outside; she loved to chase butterflies and lie in the swing. She was spoiled to the house, however, and was perfectly content living the pampered, soft life of a lady. Wong and Kit thanked God every night for bringing her into their lives. They also prayed heartily for Mrs. Witherspoon and the family, as they had been the key to Wong and Kit's happiness here in Mississippi. They could see that time was taking its toll on Mrs. Witherspoon's health, and many of their prayers centered on the topic of giving her everlasting life. It had never been discussed with them whether they would have a place when Mrs. Witherspoon passed.

One night in early May, Mrs. Witherspoon told the story of the Bell Witch, and since that evening Wong and Kit had experienced some mysterious things happening in the household. They swore to each other that food was disappearing from the kitchen. Sometimes it was cake or pie that would be missing pieces; sometimes it was an item inexplicably found in a different location in the house. They kept their mouths shut, however, fearing that discussion of these things with the family might bring them bad luck.

One thing Grandmother Witherspoon would not do was scare the children with her storytelling; it was important for them not to have nightmares or unexplained questions about their lives or their heritage. So when asked by Amanda to tell about the Bell Witch, she was careful to make sure the children knew the story was only an old tale that had never been proven true.

She explained that this legend was as prevalent in Tennessee and Mississippi because the families of two of John Bell's children moved from North Carolina to Tennessee, and later to Mississippi in the 1830s. In fact, it was said that the Bell family moved to Mississippi to rid themselves of the witch.

In Tennessee, the Bell children were tumbled from their beds at least once a week and woke the next morning with every stitch of their bedclothes snatched off and their hair all tangled and mussed up.

She noted that the story had been told in many renditions as time passed. The legend was probably embellished and changed along the way. So people might hear one version of the story today and a different one tomorrow.

Apparently it was believed that this witch made the Bell family miserable by doing many mean, tortuous, and disturbing things.

One day the Bells were going to church in their horse-pulled wagon. Suddenly it came to a stop, and they tried everything they could to get the horses to move the wagon forward, to no avail. All at once, the witch lifted the wagon, transported it through the air for a short distance, and then placed it on the ground again, with all persons and horses unharmed.

One of the Bells' girls was the victim of most of the mean happenings, and she eventually grieved her life away.

Once, the girl was getting ready for a party, combing her hair, and suddenly her hair was full of cockleburs. She broke the comb, and she cried when she couldn't get them out. The witch yelled to the girl, saying she did not want her to go to the party. The menfolk in the house came in and shot guns at the windows. The windows didn't break, and the bullets returned to the pockets of their vests.

No one ever saw it, but lots of times members of the family would see food items come out of the cupboard on their own. The witch's favorite was cream, and she would skim all the cream off the tops of all the pans in the springhouse. They were never able to make butter.

When the Bell family hired a nasty overseer who abused their poor black slaves, the Bell crops that year were a failure: bumblebee cotton, scraggly tobacco, and nubbin corn. Their mules died of colic, and the cows and hogs got sick of something incurable. They had to sell all their slaves and move.

She paused to say that there were many more stories but that she felt they got the gist of the witch's behavior. After the Bell girl died, the witch never returned.

Grandmother looked at the grandchildren, who were wide awake and alert after the story. Most times, she would notice at least one of them nod off a little.

She called for hot chocolate before bed. After all, cotton harvest time was here, and the kids would be back to Grandma's more often till the end of harvest. Amanda and the kids often spent the day with Grandma while Charles was managing the harvest. This year, however, the harvest would not be very productive because of damage from the hurricane. Charles had already discussed with Mrs. Witherspoon that they had a choice to take production or a tax credit—whichever was more beneficial.

The Witherspoon Cotton Plantation

To the world, Mississippi was the epicenter of the cotton production industry phenomenon during the first half of the nineteenth century. Mrs. Witherspoon's descendants built their wealth from cotton. Cotton gave the South power, both real and imagined.

In the past, many early settlers in the colonies grew cotton and used slaves to complete the tedious work of picking, ginning (deseeding), and baling the cotton. With slavery, field slaves worked the crops; house slaves tended to the plantation owner and his family. After the invention of the cotton gin, plantation owners found themselves in a position to produce and sell much more cotton than ever before, and demand for slaves skyrocketed.

Slavery was deeply woven into the entire Southern economy, culture, and lifestyle. Rich whites owned slaves; however, a small number of freedmen and never-enslaved African Americans were also slaveholders. Typical plantations had anywhere from nine or ten to twenty-five slaves. Today, however, it was a new ball game. Hired help to pull off several harvests was now hard to find and was not as reliable with no allegiance to the farm.

Cotton production soared from 156,000 bales in 1800 to more than 4,000,000 bales in 1860. (A bale is a compressed bundle of cotton weighing between four hundred and five hundred pounds). Thank goodness for modern technology; if one managed one's production properly, one could work with less labor. Some skilled machine operators were a must. There were numbers of workers who followed crop production to make a living; this was where Charles had to manage the day-to-day operation in hands-on fashion to keep production moving.

The Witherspoon Cotton Plantation consisted of over 300 acres, 260 of which were reserved for cotton production. This was considered enough acreage to be considered a plantation. The harvesting season would last about two months. More than one picking usually occurred as the bolls ripened.

On the plantation were buildings to house the equipment (including a cotton gin and, often, a cotton press). The outbuildings were used to support worker functions. They included kitchens, washhouses. workers' quarters, and privies. Years before, a row of slave quarters stood behind the plantation house—cabins and an overseer's house. The slaves' cabins were roughly made and lacked any features of comfort. They had dirt floors and lacked proper doors and windows, and the furniture was limited to what the slaves could make. These had been updated to accommodate a more sheltered camp approach for workers. At harvest time now, Wong would go with Charles to the fields and cook for the crew every day.

Not every plantation had a great and elegant mansion house. The typical plantation house was a one-or one-and-one-half-story cottage with a columned gallery. Such was the case with the Witherspoon house. The Witherspoon house, however, was architecturally elaborate, with many extra comfort features were installed.

Handpicking cotton is the best method of obtaining fully grown cotton, because unwanted material, called "trash", such as leaves and the remains of immature bolls, would be left behind for the second or third picking.

After the harvested cotton has been dried and much of the trash removed, the fibers are separated from their seeds in a process called ginning. The cotton gin separates the fiber and the seeds mechanically; it is able to separate fifty pounds per day. Following separation, the cotton is pressed into bales and wrapped for protection. The seeds are not wasted but are used to make cotton seed oil and food for cattle. As the bales come off the gin press, a gin employee uses a cookie-cutter type of tool to remove a sample from each bale. Each sample is identified as being from a particular bale.

The next step is classing, during which the quality of the cotton is decided. It is judged by the hand and eye. The value of cotton depends on the length of the fiber, its color, its feel, and the amount of remaining trash in it. Once the quality of a bale is decided, the price is set and the cotton is taken to the market. It is sold to a cotton merchant, who sells the cotton to mills.

Unlike other farm products, cotton is not perishable and can be stored for a long time. Sometimes farmers store the bales until they can receive a more favorable price. Every day, faxes came into Charles's office with the most up-to-date prices of cotton.

As with all other crops, contracts for cotton quantity and terms are audited. Most contracts are stated in bales; therefore, the yield per acre (in pounds) needs to be converted to bales (at five hundred pounds per bale). As all the cotton is not always sold at the same time, a yield comparison is essential to ensure that all bales are accounted for with sales contracts.

Sales contracts have a variety of options: price later contracts, pricing by grade contracts, option contracts, and deferred payment contracts.

As the plantation would someday belong to Douglas, he was allowed to come with Charles on some days and observe the work. There was a lot of work with heavy machinery, so Charles was careful to protect Douglas from this part of the harvesting to prevent injury.

This year, Douglas begged for two days and nights for Hoss to come along to the fields during harvest. He won the battle, and every day after Amanda brought him home from school, Charles would pick up Douglas and Hoss to go to the fields. Douglas was instructed to keep Hoss with him at all times.

This was a particular treat for Hoss, as he had been a couch potato for a couple of months at the Witherspoon household. He jumped up and down like a child when approaching the truck to go to the fields. He would ride in the back with his nose to the wind and his feet steady on the bed of the truck.

At first, Hoss was pretty good about staying near Douglas. But after the comfort zone passed, he would wander off to participate in his old shenanigans of hunting in the woods. Douglas would run up and down the area, frantically calling for Hoss to return, and he always did—but only when Hoss was ready. Charles warned Douglas that if Hoss went near the machinery, he would not get to come anymore. Luckily that was not what interested Hoss.

One day a worker fell from the gin, and his leg was seriously injured. Charles always tried to get his workers to wear work boots, but sometimes help was hard to find. In today's labor options, Charles was forced to take anyone he could get. He had a very diverse labor pool of blacks, Mexicans, Chinese and a few whites. Unless Charles wanted to buy the boots for everyone, chances that the workers would all have boots were slim to none.

Lunchtime at the offsite kitchen was always a cheery time for the workers, who loved Wong's cooking and looked forward to lying under a tree or squatting to eat. Precisely at 12:00 noon, everyone collected. Depending on how far from the fields the workers were coming from, the timing of workers coming in a staggering way allowed for no waste of time in line to eat. Charles, Douglas, and Hoss ate in the kitchen at a table away from the workers. Charles took all precautions to protect his son from any ill play or vulgar behavior from the migrant workers. On weekends, Douglas was pleased to get an all-day experience in the fields.

At lunch Charles took the time to discuss some of the day's work with Douglas to better educate him every year. One of his thoughts this year in school was to have Douglas study the cotton plant and the evolution of its growth through the season till harvest. Perhaps Douglas would have a paper to do that would fit in. After that, he wanted Douglas to know more about what happened to the cotton when it left the fields, and the benefits of cotton to society.

Charles told Douglas that Eli Whitney was inspired by a cat to invent the cotton gin. Eli witnessed a cat pulling bird feathers through a cage and quickly associated that action with the possibility of mechanically removing seeds from cotton with a combing mechanism. Charles added that a lot of people didn't know that, and he further explained that Eli Whitney had been a tutor on a plantation.

During harvest time, when Wong was out preparing lunch for the workers, Kit took over food preparation for the house. Over the years, Mrs. Witherspoon had taught Kit how to make homemade biscuits, gravy, grits, turnip greens, and fried children in the southern tradition. In fact, occasionally during the year, Mrs. Witherspoon would request a southern meal, and Kit would proudly pull out her iron skillets, ready to make Mrs. Witherspoon smile.

Angel continued to be the center of Kit's attention, and when she cooked, Angel was in the kitchen; when she cleaned, Angel wasn't far behind. This was, of course, around the little naps that Angel would seize in Kit's bedroom. She loved to curl up on the blanket and have a quiet place to go. All in all, Angel was a pampered baby, and everyone went along with the idea. Even Tiffany got bored with Angel's constant vigil with Kit.

Tonight a southern meal awaited the family. The aroma of the fried chicken and biscuits filled the air. At harvest time, dinner was later than normal in the evenings. The workers stayed in the fields as long as there was light. Dinner, a little wind-down time after eating, and sleep were the order of the day.

How the Boll Weevil Got to Mississippi

Grandma's story tonight related to the cotton plantation. Douglas had been interested in the pheromone traps in the fields and what their function was.

"Although the boll weevil is now gone from Mississippi, it is not forgotten. Boll Weevils are insects capable of long-duration flight and can move surprising distances when carried by the winds. Some studies have captured marked boll weevils sixty-three to one hundred sixty-nine miles from the point where they were released.

"One of the distinguishing characteristics of the boll weevil is its elongated snout. This one characteristic does not, however, mean the beetle is definitely a boll weevil, as there are more than four hundred species of weevils in Mississippi, such as pecan weevils and billbugs.

"Boll weevils vary in size from one-eighth to one-third of an inch. Newly emerged boll weevils are reddish brown in color, while older weevils are usually gray.

"The body of an adult boll weevil is sparsely covered with small, light-colored hairs, being especially dense around its thorax. The hairs just behind the head create the appearance of a light-colored stripe; this is a useful characteristic when examining the weevil.

"The best way to distinguish boll weevils from other weevils in Mississippi is to examine the largest segment of the front leg. It is large and club-shaped, with two distinct spurs on the inside or bottom edge of the club, with the innermost spur being about twice as long as the outer one.

"Boll weevils have to develop and reproduce in cotton; therefore, it was not until Mississippi's cotton production was established that the weevil was able to invade and thrive here. They first entered the United States through Texas and by 1907 had traveled to the Natchez area, damaging crops. Therefore, from the time the weevil first entered the US until it infested the entire eastern cotton belt, it spread at a rate of about fifty-five miles per year. It took only seven years for the weevil to spread throughout the state of Mississippi.

"Both male and female boll weevils cause feeding damage by using their small mandibles located at the end of their snouts to chew into the fruit and feed on the inner portion of the cotton boll. This creates a small hole in the fruit known as a feeding puncture.

"After feeding inside a boll, female boll weevils usually deposit a single egg into the feeding puncture. Before leaving the hole, she seals the hole with a glue-like substance, which creates a pimple-like scar. Within a few days after the egg hatches, the small boll weevil grub feeds on the interior of the boll. Within a few days, the bolls normally shed from the plant and fall to the ground. The remainder of the larva's development is completed inside the boll. In four to seven days, the adult weevil chews its way from the boll and begins to attack more bolls. A boll weevil can complete all four stages of its life cycle in about three weeks.

"Losses caused by boll weevils in Mississippi exceeded 5 percent in some years, the highest years of damage being 1987–1989. Cotton growers annually fund the Boll Weevil Eradication Maintenance Program, with the key component of preventative measures being maintenance of the pheromone traps. The traps have to be properly maintained and run on a regular basis. If a field is found to be infested, it receives prompt insecticide treatments along with extension of the program throughout the area."

Grandma Witherspoon closed her story to nodding heads by saying that nothing since the boll weevil had caused such damage to cotton farmers until Hurricane Katrina.

Everyone kissed Grandma for her everlasting passion to pass on important information indigenous to Mississippi. Without her tireless work over the years at the historical society, she would not have all this wonderful history to share. She felt, as part of her agenda, this was one of the best things she could do for her family and their futures.

When Douglas was in the house, Hoss slept in his bed. They were buddies through and through, and Douglas did not look forward to the day when harvest was over and he would be leaving Grandma's house. Tonight, Hoss was sticky with spurs and burrs from the fields. Douglas reminded himself that tomorrow evening, he would brush out Hoss's coat.

Hoss was happy here in his new home, but he had some habitual needs as an outside dog to engage in some behaviors that Charles and Douglas did not approve of and this confused Hoss. His former family never disciplined him for bringing home a rabbit or killing a squirrel. Douglas had taken the place of Ben; Hoss loved Douglas. But he still had that wild hair every now and then when he was out in the fields to run free, sniff out varmints, and follow the hunt.

The End of Harvest Brings Bad News

On a chilly October evening, Charles paid his workers after all the work had been completed; the cotton had been loaded on trucks with trailers, and all the machinery had been maintained and stored. He breathed a sigh of relief and was the last one out of the fields. He started down the road to the truck to go home. He was really confused about where he had left the truck, because it wasn't where he thought he left it. After a few minutes, he was angry and disappointed to realize that the truck had been stolen right from his own fields, probably by a migrant worker having been paid and finished with his work. He remembered that Douglas's schoolbooks and sweater were still in the truck, and a small amount of cash he had not needed was locked in the glove compartment. Little did he know that Hoss had also been in the truck when it was stolen. He often napped in the seat, taking in the sun and its lazy day.

Charles trekked several miles home after dark; the family was beginning to worry about him. Douglas had stayed home that night and was busy with his grandmother and house activities, unaware that Hoss was not in the house. Hoss had meandered back near the truck later. The migrant worker stealing the truck was so anxious to get out of the area that he didn't bother to dump the dog.

After returning home, Charles explained why he was late and the problem at hand. He quietly told the ladies about Hoss. He wasn't ready to deal with Douglas about the loss of the dog and his schoolbooks. He promptly called the local police.

An all-points bulletin was released to the news media as well as all Mississippi police departments.

***

Hoss was now companion to a fugitive on the run. He had no idea he was in trouble. He loved riding in the truck and was living for the moment.

Javier was headed to Biloxi to board his brother's coaster ship, which was headed up the coast, loaded with shrimp. He had only about thirty miles to cover on highway 49 to get to Gulfport, where he would pick up highway 10. If he could stay ahead of the police in the camouflage of darkness, he would get to Biloxi during the night, ditch the truck, and board the boat to leave the next morning.

Javier drove fast with a purpose and occasionally talked to the dog. He loved dogs and was familiar with Hoss's personality from watching him in the fields. He was a good dog; Maybe Manuel would allow him to bring Hoss onto the boat.

When Javier stopped for gas, he stole a license plate off a parked car in the lot and changed the plates on the truck. Hoss took a pee and was coaxed back into the truck by Javier. Javier used this stop to pick up dinner from McDonald's; he ordered a cheeseburger for Hoss.

***

While Javier and Hoss rode along in the darkness, the family at home was extremely upset and worried about Hoss. Charles did not lose much from the loss of the truck, and Douglas's books could be replaced. It was Hoss who was on everyone's mind. Grandmother Witherspoon had a panic attack and had to go to bed. Douglas shut himself in the bedroom, sobbing and feeling guilty and responsible. Everyone else just went through the motions of the evening, staying alert to any news. After nearly midnight, Charles and Amanda decided everyone had to get some sleep before daybreak. Everyone was ordered to bed.

***

Javier and Hoss pulled into Biloxi in the evening. Javier went straight to the pier to make his connection. He parked the truck in a secluded area and walked down to the pier with Hoss. Manuel saw him coming and threw up his hand in greeting. Hoss tagged along beside Javier. Manuel called out, "Who's your friend?" Javier told his brother that he was a stray that he had adopted just the week before. He said he had named him Hoss and asked if he could come along on the trip. Manuel wouldn't commit yet but said he would think about it.

The shrimp Manuel was carrying up the coast was produced locally, though the load was sparse because of the hurricane. Manuel had worked on the double-rigged trawlers, harvesting mostly brown shrimp, before he got his own ship.

The shrimp industry has been a vital part of Mississippi's coastal development. While gaming and tourism are Biloxi's most important industry, the seafood industry contributes hundreds of millions of dollars to the Gulf Coast economy. There are thirty-eight seafood processing plants situated along the Gulf Coast, with eleven in Biloxi.

Building boats and producing boat paraphernalia are also big businesses in the area, employing about ten thousand workers.

Javier and Hoss were invited to bed down on the boat that night to prepare for the next day's excursion. They boarded the boat and went straight down to bed. Manual told Javier to be thinking about how Hoss's waste would be handled on the boat—an important element in the sanitation procedures.

Javier slept in a bunk with Hoss by his bed. He wasn't invited onto the bunk, as the space was limited.

The next morning, Javier woke with enthusiasm that he had the answer to Hoss's waste issue. He would build a small sandbox of sorts at the end and corner of one of the decks and fill it with mulch or sawdust and maintain its cleanliness. Manual seemed to be okay with this, and Javier spent the morning getting his materials together with Hoss close behind. Javier even bought a small shrub (which would certainly die) to go in the box so that Hoss would have something to hoist his leg on.

***

The family back home was notified that Charles's truck had been found in Biloxi, near the pier. His cash was still in the locked glove box, along with Douglas's books and sweater. There was no information on the whereabouts of the dog or the migrant worker, the name of which was unknown.

The grieving continued with the family, but Charles took his family home and resumed daily business. Grandmother Witherspoon prayed for Hoss and sank into depression.

The Green Dragon

The fifty-foot Florida Bay Coaster *Green Dragon* left on a chilly, overcast morning in October. Cold rain misted from the slate-gray sky, and a brisk wind blew robustly from the east. Coasters are small cargo ships, often container ships, that run on feeder routes. That is, they carry a relatively small number of containers from small ports to major ports. They are called coasters because they travel along the coast, making many stops in a short period.

Hoss was all atwitter. He had never been on a sea vessel before and was nervous to say the least. Javier thought it best to shut Hoss in the cabin during shove-off, as there would be much activity on the deck.

It was a nice boat with a pilothouse, raised master bedroom, covered rear deck, medium deck, and head/shower. It was double-bunked for the crew and had a cozy saloon along with the essential galley.

The *Green Dragon* was loaded with brown shrimp and supplies to make the coastal journey up to Texas and Mexico and back, stopping at several ports along the way.

Except for going into port and departing, life on the ship was relaxed and unstructured. It was not a bad life if one had the itch to travel. Adventure was the name of the game, and every day was a new day filled with new business and new challenges. Except for the fear of really bad weather and high seas, the trips were easy and brought easy money for the crew.

With a small crew of four, the cook, the captain, and the pilot, everyone built new relationships. When everything was relaxed and slow, sometimes the pilot would show the crew the pilothouse and give short lessons on steering a course, navigating (including during a fog), and general handling of the boat. Tying knots was a big thing with the crew, and novice sailors were kept busy learning.

The crew played a lot of cards, read, and slept in their off time. The food was usually very good, consisting of a variety of items including beef, pork, and veal dishes; hash; stew; ragout; soups; a variety of breads, including hoecakes and biscuits; pastries; puddings; omelets; and sweets. Workers usually gained a few pounds during these excursions.

The cook was a crusty old man named Nam who had cooked on ships for twenty-seven years after he left the army. He dared anyone to criticize the food and took no suggestions or requests for special dishes. Nonetheless, everyone always ended up falling in love with the old guy, as he loved to cook and was very good at it. He ignored all compliments and shrugged off most conversation. However, after a good compliment, the person who had given it would probably (if Nam was having a good day) get an extra spoonful during the next meal.

The pilot was a retired coast guard pilot who knew his stuff. Antonio had been through many a bad sea and somehow always came out on top. He'd had a few close calls but chalked it up to God's will that he was still piloting—the passion and love of his life. He'd never had a wife or kids because he never wanted to leave family for his career, which took him away almost all the time. He was the eldest child in his family, and he had basically raised his three brothers and sister while his negligent parents were rarely home. He said he never wanted kids of his own, and he kept to his word. His sense of responsibility caused him to always give 100 percent of his effort to his work.

Manuel had worked hard all his life and enjoyed being the "chosen son" of his parents in Mexico. However, he often would think of his stray brother and wish things were different. After all, they were still brothers. Manuel's parents were affluent people who owned real estate in Cabo San Lucas. When Cabo was discovered as *the* place to go, real estate soared and made the family a great deal of money. They had two sons, Manuel and Javier.

Manuel had finished a course of study at a community college in San Diego and from that point wanted his own business. He did not want to further his education; he felt it was a waste. He was ready for a "real" job. When he met and married a girl from Mississippi, he discussed moving to her hometown after she finished school. Manuel's parents provided the start-up money for him to buy a boat and go into business for himself. He later joined with a company in order to get regular business from the coastal trade in Mississippi.

Javier had been a troubled youth since he was twelve years old. He left home at fifteen to avoid the pressures of measuring up to his parents' expectations. He was not as smart as Manuel and always felt inferior. He got into trouble often enough to continually avoid the law and did only cash jobs that would allow him his anonymity. He had not seen his parents once since he had left home and heard indirectly from his brother that he was a "forgotten" son, as he had disgraced his parents.

Javier always could count on running with his brother when he needed cash or could be in Biloxi at the right time, according to the ship's departure schedule. Javier and Manuel enjoyed seeing each other but did not delve into each other's lives. Javier could feel comfortable that he didn't have to list his activities or tell Manuel how he lived.

One important stipulation had been made in the beginning, however. Though Javier was always welcome to come, he had to come on as a crew member just like the rest of the crew and respect his brother's position as captain of the ship. Most of the time, he never told the crew they were brothers.

The crew on this particular job consisted of three additional crew members besides Javier. With three crew cabins, that left Javier with one to himself and Hoss.

The other three crew members were part-timers who picked up work with Manuel and other ships sporadically as they needed work. Two were alcoholics who used these jobs every now and then to sober up enough to make a little money. The last crew member was a young man of about twenty-four doing a research study on coastal shrimping.

With the *Green Dragon* was out to sea and on its way, Javier let Hoss out of the cabin and into the sea air. Hoss didn't have his sea legs as he tried to walk around and follow Javier, but he loved the air. He pointed his nose to the wind with his tail standing up and his four legs planted as steadily as possible and deeply took in the smells of the sea. Javier tried to make him comfortable with his new home by petting him a lot and introducing him to the crew. Everyone was excited about having a dog on board. Hoss was like a mascot to everyone. Even the cook was civil to him.

Hoss especially enjoyed going into the pilothouse and perching on a chair to look out at the ocean. He also felt more comfortable in the pilothouse and quickly made friends with Antonio.

The sandbox worked fine; Hoss was used to being outside, so having it on the deck seemed natural to him. Before Hoss became 100 percent comfortable with the box, he did mark a lot of the outside decks. No one said anything, and the crew just took care of it as they swabbed.

Hoss had become a very adaptable dog after the hurricane and thankfully lived for the day. As long as he was being fed and had people to love him, he was happy. Now Hoss was a sailor, and everyone on the ship was proud of him as their official mascot. Someone even tied a nautical kerchief around Hoss's neck to anoint him an official member of the crew. Sometimes when he was in the pilothouse, Antonio would put his pilot's cap on Hoss for a few minutes.

The crew member doing the research study on shrimping, Dave, was especially enamored with Hoss and wrote a couple of newsworthy articles about him during the trip that he planned to release to the press. He knew the public would love hearing this story. He was able to get a few candid snapshots of Hoss wearing his kerchief on deck with his nose to the wind. Wow, what a dog!

Antonio heard about Dave's camera and invited him to the pilothouse to get a picture of Hoss in the pilot's chair while wearing the hat. They were even able to get Hoss to put his paw on the steering wheel. Hoss was fast becoming the crew's favorite pastime, and Hoss was enjoying all the attention.

The food was better than good, the affection from all the men was more than Hoss had ever received, and Hoss was beginning to love his job. Every day, he was to participate in the delivery of printed information coming into the pilothouse to the captain. The pilot trained him to take the rolled-up documents on weather and daily shrimp prices, as well as any other faxes that came through, to Manuel's cabin twice a day. He scratched on the master bedroom door, delivered his paperwork, and was rewarded with a piece of jerky. He slept in Javier's cabin; he had acquired his own blanket from the extra bunk and was as cozy as a bedbug. Life was good.

The ship was headed for its first port in Texas on the third day at sea when complications disrupted the excursion.

On the Road Again

One morning, Javier felt serious stomach pains and nausea. He tried to have breakfast but couldn't keep it down. Hoss could tell something was wrong and was concerned. He stayed in the cabin with Javier to offer support.

Apparently Javier's appendix had ruptured, and he was in serious trouble. After conferring with his brother, who radioed a doctor with the symptoms, he learned that he had to get to a hospital as soon as possible.

The coast guard was notified of the emergency and caught up to the *Green Dragon* four hours later. Javier was taken on board to go to the nearest hospital, and of course, Hoss was with him. The coast guard couldn't believe his dog had been on the ship, but they reacted professionally to get them both off the ship and to the nearest hospital.

Manuel felt terrible to see Javier go through this trauma, but he was glad to get the coast guard's assistance and be able to continue with his trip to stay on schedule. Everyone prayed for Javier and missed Hoss sorely.

Javier was rushed to the nearest hospital in Galveston, Texas, and the question remained about what to do with Hoss. Hoss had warmed up to one of the coast guard crew, Scott, and it was decided that Scott would foster Hoss until he could be with his owner. This was extremely lucky for Hoss, as the normal procedure would have been for him to go to the shelter.

Scott did not have a dog, but his family had been begging for one; this good deed with Hoss would provide a little perk for them. Hoss went with Scott after Javier was delivered to the hospital, and he again began a new adjustment to new people and new surroundings.

While Javier was being transported to the hospital, it was learned through reports that Javier was wanted in several states for theft and drug charges, which put another spin on the new foster situation with Scott. Scott took Hoss home with him in Galveston, bonded with him, made him as comfortable as he could, and waited to see what happened. It appeared that Javier would be going from the hospital to jail to address his outstanding warrants, and now life for Hoss was uncertain.

After several days of fostering Hoss, Scott's family fell fast in love with him and his adaptable spirit and loving personality. It was determined that Hoss was a very special dog, and time would tell what avenue he would go down next.

Scott had one child, a nine-year-old boy named Christian, who became instantly attached to Hoss, and of course this complicated everything. Scott had decisions to make about Hoss's future.

In the meantime, Christian and Hoss were fast friends, and Hoss was not entirely uncomfortable with the arrangement. He was just a little confused about the transition.

Scott had a friend in the local police department who worked with trained canines used for tracking and general police work related to crimes and disappearances of individuals.

He invited his friend over to meet Hoss. Scott's friend gave Hoss a basic screening test required to evaluate his qualifications for police training in the canine unit. There was no question after a forty-five-minute evaluation that Hoss might be accepted into the police academy in Houston and, after training at the academy, be screened for important work with the police department.

Hoss left with the policeman, Jack, and within the next two days was transferred to Houston and accepted into the novice program to begin his training for police work.

This was a new challenge for Hoss, but he was treated well and did not feel threatened. At this point, Hoss had gotten used to change and adapted well to moving. The one consistent thing that stayed with Hoss was his loving spirit and affectionate personality. Without this, Hoss perhaps would not have even survived up to this point.

The Academy

Police dogs live with their partners. Hoss was assigned to Sean, a young new officer fresh from police school. Hoss and Sean had something in common; they were both green regarding police experience.

Sean and Hoss took to each other right away. Sean lived alone. He was an adopted orphan and had taken care of himself since the age of eighteen. He had always wanted to become a police officer and had worked like a Trojan for eight years to get into this position—that of a fully trained new officer ready for the streets with the canine unit. Only the most dedicated officers are considered for K-9 units. They must have exemplary records; an outgoing, energetic personality; and strong physical conditioning. A K-9 officer often puts in sixty hours each week. The pay is good, but the schedule is grueling, and there's no backing out once the commitment is made. A police dog's career usually lasts about six years, but the handler must be in it for the long haul.

Sean was motivated and ecstatic about his work; at the same time, he had some butterflies about the newness of the K-9 unit. He had heard that butterflies were a healthy sign; otherwise the person was not serious about their training. He was tough on the outside but wore a beautiful wide grin that melted the hearts of everyone who met him.

Police departments obtain dogs from a variety of sources. Some are donated by their original owners; however, now police departments are realizing the importance of using dogs that have been specifically bred for police work. Dogs that aren't bred for the work have to measure up against a core set of physical attributes and meet specific criteria.

No one is quite sure when humans first domesticated dogs, but one thing is certain—dogs and people have been working side by side for thousands of years. Modern training methods have led to dogs becoming integral parts of many people's lives not just as companions but also as guide dogs, search-and-rescue dogs, and bomb-or drug-sniffing dogs. But few dogs are asked to give as much of themselves as police dogs.

The history of police dogs goes back to when European police forces were using bloodhounds, as early as the eighteenth century. It wasn't until World War I that countries like Belgium and Germany formalized the training process and started using dogs for specific tasks, such as guard duty. The practice continued through World War II. Soldiers returning home brought news of the well-trained dogs being used by both sides of the conflict. Soon, K-9 programs were established in London and other cities across Europe. The use of police dogs didn't gain a foothold in the United States until the 1970s. Today police dogs are recognized as a vital part of law enforcement, and the use of police dogs has grown rapidly in the last few years.

Today police forces in most major cities use police dogs to track criminals, sniff out illegal materials, search buildings, and do other jobs human police officers can't do as well as dogs can. Not only are there thousands of police dogs on the job on a given day, but there are also hundreds of police dogs who have given their lives to protect and serve their communities.

Why do police departments bother using police dogs at all? For one thing, their sense of smell is almost fifty times more sensitive than a human's. In addition to sensitivity, a dog's sense of smell is precise. It can discern a specific scent even when there are dozens of other scents around. Drug smugglers have tried to fool drug-sniffing dogs by wrapping drugs in towels soaked in perfume, but the dogs find the drugs anyway.

Sean and Hoss began basic training on the following Monday. Hoss had been with Sean for three nights and one full day before training began. Sean prayed that both he and Hoss would measure up to the stringent training required to make it through the academy. Hoss had a threatening look about him but was a loving, considerate dog judging by what Sean could observe. He was not as big as some of his counterparts but was strongly built, with good bone structure and a good nose. He could only hope his times in the wild had given him some other attributes that could be embellished as a police dog.

Hoss had to first become an expert at basic obedience training. He needed to obey the commands of his handler, Sean, without hesitation. Such obedience is what keeps the inherent aggression of a police dog in check and allows the officer to control how much force the dog is using against a suspect.

Hoss also had to make it through endurance and agility training. He had to be able to jump over walls and climb stairs. He needed to be acclimated to city life, because a dog that is nervous around people won't make a good police dog.

Finally, if Hoss made it through all this training, he would go through some type of specialty training. Many dogs are trained to search for drugs, though some are bomb or gun sniffers. Police dogs can also track missing persons, dead people, or criminal suspects.

On the first day of obedience training, the dogs and handlers were split into teams of six to eight dogs per team. The dogs who had not previously been worked on a leash were put into a smaller group; Hoss and Sean were in this group.

Lots of leash walking in circles occurred, with corrections made when the dog walked too far in front of the handler or too far in back. Having the dog walk comfortably on the lead at a natural pace on the handler's left and at his side was the goal. All dog training was done in a positive manner with treats and praise.

During the day, the dogs learned to execute a right turn in motion, a left turn in motion, and an about-turn in motion. Corrective walking continued for almost the full day. Sean felt good about Hoss's responsiveness. Half of the next day would be spent on these exercises, and any dog who did not listen to his handler or respond positively to treats and positive correction was immediately weeded out. One dog from Hoss's team left the school after the second day.

The second half of the second day was devoted to training the dogs to stand, sit, or lie down in motion, with a recall to heel. These were four separate maneuvers that had to be learned by the end of the third day. Each day, a small review would take place first, and then the new material would be introduced. At this point, the dogs were performing off lead and had to be superbly tuned in to their handler and his commands.

You have to understand that what a normal dog would learn in eight one-hour sessions spread over eight weeks, these dogs learned all day long. It was an exhausting process both for the dogs and the handlers—especially in the beginning, when everyone was trying to get over the fear of failure. The handlers were being trained first and foremost that they were the leader of the pack and were the ones being trained to train the dogs. Sean's self-confidence and love for his dog showed. Hoss responded well. He liked the work. He was exuberant about the positive reward system.

At night, when Hoss and Sean would go home, they both wanted only food and rest. They were both mentally and physically drained. Hoss and Sean were bonding fast. Hoss was loving the attention and the work. He now had a job with lots of positive reinforcement—something he always longed for.

The fourth and fifth days were spent honing the exercises and testing the dogs' attention levels. While the dogs worked the field, three civilian-dressed individuals would walk passively around the field at the direction of the master instructor. This kind of diversion training was an important part of the exercise.

Additionally, gunfire (using blank ammunition) was employed after the team finished group exercises. The dogs had to remain stable during the shooting, acting neither fearful nor aggressive.

On Friday evening, when the dogs filed off the field with their handlers, everyone was feeling accomplished and happy about the first week. A new sense of confidence-building had taken place for both the dogs and the handlers. It was like a shot of adrenaline after winning a big game.

Now everyone looked forward to two days of rest and relaxation. Sean longed for a cold beer and a pillow on the couch in front of the television. That is exactly what he got, along with a pizza and a happy, attentive Hoss at his feet. Hoss and Sean were now a team; there was a deeper bond between them than was normal for an owner and his pet. They both had won a small lottery this week, having made it through phase one of boot camp, and nothing could take that great feeling from them.

Sean took Hoss with him everywhere he could. The grocery store was the only place this weekend that Hoss had to wait in the car. Sean was careful to secure the car so Hoss could not get out and no one could interact with him. It was important for the handlers to continue their "leader of the pack" routines in all phases of their relationship.

On Sunday, Sean and Hoss went fishing. Being out in the wild allowed Hoss to think about some of his former experiences. He sniffed out everything possible but was quick to return to Sean's side when recalled.

They enjoyed grilled smallmouth bass for dinner. Hoss loved the flavor of fish and could not get enough. He finished filling his stomach with the dog kibble that was in his bowl before retiring to the living room.

Monday morning, Sean and Hoss loaded up for the academy and prepared for week two.

The canine teams had to be able to demonstrate agility by surmounting obstacles on command. The obstacles could be navigated on or off lead, but the canine team had to clear the obstacles without physical assistance from the handler.

The first day was devoted to jumping hurdles of increasing height on the left, right, and center of the field. The handler introduced hand signals along with verbal commands to show left, right, and center. Hoss really liked this exercise and seemed to have fun with all the praise he was getting for running and jumping hurdles.

Throughout the week, obstacles such as a four-foot-high chain link fence, a three-foot-high structure-type window, and a vehicle window the size of that of a passenger car were introduced and worked into the training.

Several dogs encountered bumps, bruises, and abrasions, but not a single dog stopped the exercise. Appropriate breaks were given to attend to any physical issues the dogs had. Even though there were larger dogs in the class than Hoss, he was just as agile as they were. He had lost several pounds from the previous week's work, and it helped him jump higher than he would normally have jumped. Sean's grin got bigger and bigger as the week progressed while he watched an amazing group of dogs respond so positively to agility training.

If Hoss and Sean had felt tired last Friday evening, it was of no comparison to how they felt this Friday. Hoss never showed it, but he was physically sore from the jumping and was feeling the stress in his neck.

On Saturday morning, Sean picked up the phone and called a friend who owned a local spa. He explained what he was doing and asked if both he and Hoss could come for a massage. Hoss had no idea what was coming, but he tagged along normally with Sean. They were both set up in the same room on two separate massage beds. Sean commanded Hoss to lie down and stay on the bed.

What happened after that was a blur for both Sean and Hoss. Even though no oil was used on Hoss during his massage, warm stones and ten nimble fingers made him feel like a million dollars. He actually fell asleep and snored loudly for a short time.

Afterward they both went swimming in a lake to continue working their sore bodies. They went home, and Sean took Hoss into the shower with him for a good sudsing. They both smelled like lake water. Hoss had never ever had a day like this or even a shower. He was renewed and as relaxed as a limp noodle. Naptime came easily for Hoss as Sean left him to go to a movie with a friend. About the time Hoss had rested and thought he was going to burst with pee, Sean came home and let Hoss run to the nearest tree for relief.

Sean and Hoss spent Sunday visiting Sean's family. Sean explained to his mom and dad how close he and Hoss were and all the things they had accomplished in two weeks. Sean's mom fed them heartily and seemed so excited for Sean's accomplishments. They all looked at Hoss in awe and praised him abundantly with hugs and kisses. What a life! Hoss had never been so happy.

The first part of the third week was devoted to apprehension; there were two different exercises related to apprehension. First, the handler had to be protected by the dog while he was in a vehicle. The canine needed to protect the handler by coming out of the vehicle's door or window during an assault. The handler would disengage the canine by voice command only at the direction of the master instructor. This could mean that the dog would the assailant if commanded to do so. Secondly, the canine would demonstrate reasonable force during a passive or submissive encounter. The canine would be alerted on a person at a distance of at least forty yards. The person would not respond to an order to surrender, and the canine would be commanded to apprehend. As the canine approached, the person would remain nonthreatening and passive. The canine would be expected to detain the person without engagement. The handler would then recall the canine at the direction of the master instructor. Both of these exercises were to be performed in full protective clothing, with muzzles on the dogs.

It didn't take long for the dogs (some more aggressive than others) to get the idea that the commands given represented a life-and-death call to protecting his handler. There was a lot of barking and snarling, but only upon command would the dogs actually attack and bite the suspect.

It is an amazing thing to see a dog with his handler instructed to bite another man wearing protective clothing and the very next minute see the man in protective clothing pet the dog. This is where the trust of a dog is put in his handler's hands, and at all costs, he obeys the commands.

Hoss had some challenges with calming down after attacking. He actually trembled while barking when instructed to allow the suspect to pet him. Hoss was given twenty-four hours to redo this particular exercise to perfection. He was not the only dog who occasionally had to repeat an exercise. None of the dogs in Hoss's group failed an exercise after repeating it.

In the search of an open area, a canine will conduct an off-lead search for a suspect concealed in a location unknown to the team. The canine should use any means possible (tracking or air scent) to locate the suspect. The handler must notify the master instructor when the canine has located the suspect. The handler will recall the canine to a heel position at the direction of the master instructor. At least one backup officer (in addition to the master instructor) will assist the handler during the search. A verbal challenge shall be issued, and the search will be conducted in civilian clothing with the suspect hidden in a safe location. The search area is approximately one acre (such as a town lot, lumberyard, or wooded area).

The group carried out such a search exercise, and Hoss found it a lot more fun than the previous exercise. Both Sean and Hoss did well in the exercise. While Sean was sure that Hoss would protect him if he had to, neither of them had enjoyed the aggressive exercise.

Week four involved an off-lead search of a building for a suspect concealed in a location unknown to the team. The canine may use any means possible (tracking or air scent) to locate the suspect. The same procedure as searching an open area applied to this exercise. The search area was approximately five thousand square feet.

After working on the search exercise, the group was broken up to review and redo any of the exercises they had covered up to that point. Sean chose to review the chain-link fence agility exercise as well as the aggressive apprehension of an assailant. Dogs went to their respective areas to hone their skills on any possible weak points. Hoss had succeeded in the exercises, but Sean wanted to see Hoss regain his composure more quickly after the physical attack.

Obvious both to the instructors and Sean, Hoss improved his attitude during the use of physical force and then calming. He easily jumped the chain-link fence without any fumbles. Sean praised Hoss as much as he could without acting like a coach hugging an athlete who had just won a gold medal in the Olympics. Sean felt as if he were on top of the world; he was so very, very proud of his dog, Hoss.

Scent work involves both tracking and searching for evidence. The canine follows a track, unknown to the team, of a person through an open area. The track should be approximately twenty minutes old and at least four hundred yards in length when the search begins. The track shall not be a straight line. The team must locate the suspect, who may wear protective clothing for safety. The tracking exercise may be performed on or off lead.

Some of the dogs were obviously much better at this exercise than others, though all dogs eventually made their find. The exercise was repeated several times for each dog until the master instructor felt confident that the dogs had a satisfactory comfort level with tracking.

In searching for evidence, the dogs were to locate one item of evidence (knife, wallet, flashlight, handgun, etc.) that has been discarded in a grassy area. The handlers had to notify the judge when the canine had located the evidence. This exercise was to be performed on or off lead; the search area was approximately fifty square yards.

Hoss was especially good at scent work. Perhaps this was where his nomadic background gave him a head start. He had used his nose to stay alive, to eat, and to evaluate danger. Observing this exercise was exciting, as the dogs, with their noses to the ground, would move faster and faster as they came closer to their targets. Finding their target gave confidence to the dogs that they had done something good.

With week four under their belts, Sean and Hoss exuberantly went home for a weekend of rest and relaxation. Sean felt especially weary this week and wondered if Hoss did too. The weeks were adding up to a tremendous mental and physical feat to accomplish. He reminded himself, however, that they were gaining steam and moving closer to a successful training experience that would change their lives.

Sean stopped on the way home for takeout Chinese, and aside from dinner and a couple of visits to the front yard, Sean and Hoss sacked out till the next day. Hoss and Sean felt a sense of security with each other as best buds—something Sean could not remember feeling before, even with best friends. It was a scary feeling at times; it almost compared to the anxiety of a deep relationship with a woman. Hoss and Sean had invested a lot of time, energy, and confidence in each other, and the bond continued to grow stronger every day. Sean looked down at Hoss sleeping on the floor by his bed and thanked God for this golden opportunity to experience love at its best. He had given him a wonderful specimen of a dog and best friend. As he drifted off to sleep, Sean wondered about Hoss's past and felt a special respect for the dog that had been rescued off a boat with a petty criminal.

Week five came sooner than Sean had anticipated; he and Hoss would continue scent training in two more areas this week. After this week—the sixth and last week—Hoss would spend time shadowing a seasoned dog of the canine unit.

The dogs were tested on a minimum of three vehicles and two rooms in their respective environments on at least three odors, including marijuana and cocaine. All the test finds were concealed in a location unknown to the handler and would sit there for at least thirty minutes prior to the start of the testing. The test finds would weigh at least five grams. The handler would advise the master instructor when the canine had located a test find. The canine would have to locate each test find without giving a false indication.

Two full days of testing ensued, with the dogs working enthusiastically toward their finds. Two dogs falsely targeted their finds and were given twenty-four hours to be retested. Hoss was not one of these dogs, thankfully. This left the team of three dogs moving on to the next and last scent exercise.

The explosive detection dog team tested on at least five of the ten basic odors. The odors were plastic explosive, water gel, smokeless powder, black powder, sodium chlorate, potassium chlorate, commercial dynamite (ammunition based), military dynamite, trinitrotoluene, and detonating cord. Even though only five out of ten were tested, each dog was introduced to all odors at the end of testing.

Three grueling and unexciting days (at least to Sean) of this work produced 100 percent success with the team of three dogs. As the two dogs who were twenty-four hours behind the others had less time to devote to this part of the exercise, the same two dogs miscued their finds and again were given twenty-four hours to retest. This meant these two dogs were working Saturday to catch up while the other three dogs went home for the weekend.

As Sean drove home with Hoss, his thoughts raced through the week; he was relieved it was over. He was looking forward, however, to the sixth week of shadowing. He knew a couple of the officers on the canine unit and hoped he would be lucky enough to draw one of them.

During Shadow Week, Sean and Hoss were assigned to Officer Amy Whitehouse and Chico, her canine partner, both of whom were accomplished veterans. They had been together for three years. Chico, a decorated hero on the squad, was a caramel-colored boxer with an attitude. Chico lived for the chase, and Amy felt blessed to have had such a good ride with Chico. He had helped escalate her promotion to sergeant, but she felt secure about her own talents and experience. They were a team.

Amy and Chico had been on a case for three weeks now—a string of successful robberies that finally were laying down a possible pattern in the area. There was a good physical description of the three suspects, who now had robbed six regional shops and cleanly escaped. The getaway vehicles always varied and were always later found abandoned. The men were heavily armed and dangerous. Even though only a few people had been pistol-whipped and kicked, no casualties had been reported. Even so, the community was alerted that without full cooperation during armed robberies by these suspects, a shooting was very possible.

Sean and Hoss planned to shadow Amy and Chico the next day. Sean was to be in his own vehicle with Hoss, following close behind Amy and Chico. The four officers met at the precinct at 7:00 a.m. Both canines were alpha males. Both dogs were guarded, but they were tolerant of each other, staying in control under their masters' orders. Sean and Amy did not offer the dogs any unnecessary time together.

Today Sean and Hoss would follow Amy and Chico's lead. Her dog would be first to strike, if needed, and Sean would wait for Amy's command to release Hoss. Sean experienced excitement in his gut combined with a little anxiety. After all, Sean and Hoss were both rookies.

Amy knew they could have a quiet day and discussed the relaxed approach with Sean. An officer's canine feeds off his partner's body language and energy. Even though Hoss needed the training, there was no need for undue excitement. They would start with making the usual early-morning rounds patrolling their area, perhaps having coffee and doughnuts at break time. Being constantly vigilant to crime and alert to the radio gave them purpose with a serious approach to the job.

The beat was once a middle-class area of growth in the city of Houston where a lot of young families built new homes or purchased condominiums. Over the last fifteen years, these young families had predominantly moved on, giving up the neighborhoods to a lot of foreign newcomers. There was a Laotian-dominant area with its own school, church, neighborhood, and, unfortunately, gang. The Mexican population dominated the general area, with a sprinkling of Indonesians and Egyptians. The growing service industry in the city had contributed to this influx of labor to fill the positions, mostly in the large hotels. People are drawn to where jobs are and, of course, to places where they can have a better standard of living. International markets, bakeries, restaurants, cleaners, and nightclubs dotted the main artery running parallel to the neighborhood developments on either side. Every weekend, a couple of murders, a list of burglaries, and gang activity kept the local police heavily covering the area. Even a new police precinct had been added to the area several years ago.

Not all young Caucasian families had moved on from this area. Some single parents and lower-income families remained. Their children were exposed to a lot more streetwise activity than the average kid in the average neighborhood. The public schools exhibited young white boys and girls struggling to fit in within a predominantly tough-guy society. Unfortunately, some young people, especially those on the fence in intelligence and susceptibility to peer pressure, were jumping over the fence to become young hoodlums, thieves, and drug addicts. Kids at age ten started out stealing hood ornaments off cars or burglarizing their innocent neighbors. As they later began using drugs and needed steady money, even their parents and families suffered from their thievery and dishonesty. When their sons didn't pay their drug bills, their televisions may well come up missing. It was a catch-22 for single parents who struggled to make ends meet, sometimes working two jobs. They were not home to supervise their children properly or spend the needed family time together. Many of these petty thieves and addicts moved on to car break-ins, car thefts, bigger stealing opportunities, and sometimes gang violence.

Amy and Sean spent a couple of hours patrolling the area and then stopped at a Cuban bakery for coffee and pastries. The dogs were watered and relieved with a brief walk in the grassy area next to the parking lot. They moved on to the international market and made a walk through. Nothing was going on there except fairly heavy weekend shopping. Amy suggested they stop by the local hospital and check the list of emergencies from the weekend. Needless to say, there were the usual domestic violence visits, a couple of knife victims (no casualties) and, of course, the long list of common illness visits. As was the case all over the nation, people without medical insurance used the emergency rooms for medical assistance—even for the common cold. Amy jotted down the information on the knife victims and planned to follow up, time permitting. Amy suggested they get takeout for lunch and eat in the car, discussing the area.

In the middle of lunch, a call came through dispatching them to a condominium nearby where a suspected burglary was in progress. A neighbor had noticed two boys going through a back kitchen window. They sped into action and caught the two boys still in the house. Amy took the front door, and Sean the back. The boys were in the upstairs bedroom, gathering jewelry. They had already yanked out the electronics downstairs and were ready to leave. It was a simple arrest, as the boys (both around sixteen years of age) were caught red-handed and offered no resistance. They were, of course, skipping school and even lived in the same neighborhood. The owner was notified, and the two boys were taken to a juvenile correctional center for booking. Chico and Hoss didn't have to do anything except be present. Just their presence and appearance were frightening for the boys.

On the way back from the juvenile center, they received a call around 3:00 p.m. to dispatch to a local pawn shop for an armed robbery in progress. As they approached the shop and tried to cover the front door from both sides, three men came bursting out of the shop and went running wildly in three different directions. Amy directed Sean and Hoss to take the second guy, and she and Chico were quickly on foot in pursuit of the first suspect. Amy was calling for backup as she ran fearlessly toward the running man. He had reached the back alley, turned, and was headed up near several houses. Chico was hot on the man, and Amy gave him the command to bite and bring him down. The man suddenly turned and shot Chico in the head and continued running. Chico fell to the ground, bleeding profusely from the side of his head. Amy's heart stopped beating, but she couldn't stop her pursuit of the runner. Shortly thereafter, she lost her suspect and ran back to Chico. She could see he was dead and fell on the ground, sobbing with remorse.

Sean and Hoss were in heavy pursuit of the second suspect and were gaining fast. He was a smaller man and not able to run as fast as the first. As Hoss approached the suspect, Sean gave him the command to bite and apprehend. The runner was shooting wildly, trying to scare off his attackers. Hoss jumped onto his back, biting into his right shoulder, and brought him to the ground. By that time, Sean was on the scene and holding his own gun on the man. The man dropped his gun and lay on the ground, begging for the dog to stop. Hoss was pulled back but kept snarling and barking wildly at the man. Sean handcuffed the suspect and kept him on the ground as he saw help approaching. Sean and Hoss turned over the suspect to the backup officers and ran back to find Amy. They found her with police assistance and saw one of the officers covering up Chico's body with a blanket. Sean experienced a knot in his stomach and tears in his eyes as he observed Amy in a fetal position, crying uncontrollably. He was quick to console her and assist with getting her back to his car. The rest of the backup team would handle the incidents of the case and get the men to jail. He communicated with the assist team to bring Amy's car and told them he was taking her back to the precinct.

Amy begged Sean to let her stay until the ambulance picked up Chico. He didn't have the heart to say no, so they retraced their steps back to where Chico lay covered by the blanket and waited. Amy nervously talked about Chico and what a fine officer and friend he had been. It was apparent that her grief was as bad as that experienced by people who have lost a beloved family member. The ambulance arrived in about eight minutes and carried Chico back to the vehicle. He was now evidence in the case.

Who would have thought that Hoss's first day on the job would have brought blood in more ways than one.

Back at the precinct, the case was being assembled; the three men matched the descriptions of the men in the other robberies. Amy and Sean were told to hang around for reports. Police investigators were confident they could catch the third suspect and close a pretty tight case against these men.

After Amy and Sean's statements, Sean followed Amy home and asked if there was anything they could get for her or do to make her feel better. They even asked whether she wanted them to stay with her. She declined, so Sean and Hoss headed home. There was a sadness and sense of loss in the air as they went home. Sean said nothing, and Hoss lay still in the backseat.

On the way home, Sean received a call from Amy that she had changed her mind; she asked them to please come back and keep her company. Sean circled back, picked up Chinese for dinner, and entered Amy's living room while she was curled up on the sofa, still crying. Hoss approached her, and Amy hugged him close as if he were her own. They all looked at one another; the blood still on Hoss's muzzle was now on Amy and her blanket. Amy suggested Sean take a shower and use the shampoo on Hoss too. While the guys went to the shower, Amy changed blankets and shirts. Sean found the washer and put the four towels that had been used in it. He threw in the blanket and started the cycle.

Afterward, they ate the Chinese and talked about the day. Amy made Hoss a bowl of Chico's food, and everyone felt that a special bond had been formed that day between the three of them.

After dinner and a little more conversation, Sean and Hoss went home. Sean knew Amy was on a short administrative leave because of the death of her partner, so they promised to call the next day. She hugged Hoss (maybe a little too hard) and commented to Sean that he really had a good partner.

Amy thought about what a nice guy Sean was—very thoughtful, a good officer, and very comfortable to be around. He gave off calm vibrations, and this helped a lot.

That night Sean talked to Hoss like a brother. It had taken them a long time to calm down after the incident, even though everything had gone by the book. He was so proud of Hoss following his commands to the letter. He looked down on the floor beside his bed and stroked Hoss's fur. He thanked God for keeping them safe. Special prayers were said for Amy and Chico.

The next day, Sean and Hoss spent almost the entire day at the precinct. He helped plan the funeral service for Chico the next day. He also spent more time with the investigators on the case. Hoss was congratulated over and over again on his takedown.

When Sean and Hoss headed for work the next day, it was with a heavy heart, as they knew it was time for Chico's funeral. They would be with Amy and would try to offer strength and encouragement.

Chico was buried with full military honors as a canine officer who had died in the call of duty with a flawless police record. A handsome picture of Chico sitting tall at attention and showing his attitude was displayed. Amy whispered to Sean that she would not be able to start over with a new dog.

In the car, Sean promised not to mention what she had said and allow her the freedom to change her mind and to adjust. They headed to the precinct.

When they arrived and the office was somewhat back to normal, the lieutenant asked Sean, Amy, and Hoss to come into his office. They were expecting to hear from him today, as both of them needed new assignments. Lieutenant Bowman again expressed his condolences to Amy. He told Sean that Hoss would be decorated for his takedown at graduation from the academy on Friday. Sean smiled and patted Hoss on the head. Lieutenant Bowman asked Amy if she would be willing to ride with Sean the rest of this week to continue and complete Sean and Hoss's training. She liked this idea. It would give her time to think and get right back into duty. There was an added plus that she liked the company as well. She consented, and the lieutenant told them to carry on in the same area.

Amy, Sean, and Hoss left the precinct and headed to get some lunch. They reported in, giving the dispatcher their new position. After lunch, they were dispatched to a middle school where two students had been caught with drugs. Ronnie and Chris, both in the ninth grade, had been lingering in a car before school, smoking pot. They were suspended from school and taken to the juvenile center to face misdemeanor drug charges. These two young men were examples of the vulnerable neighborhood and had crossed the fence to fit in. They could have had a totally different story had they lived in a setting with the right supervision and parenting. Ronnie's mother was a widow and was not very strict about Ronnie's whereabouts. Ronnie had an inner anger that he was acting out that probably had something to do with his father's death. Chris was the victim of a divorce and did not have a father as a role model. His mother worked two jobs and left Chris alone far too much for his own good.

Hoss sniffed out the parking lot and targeted at least eight cars for marijuana. The rest of the day was spent identifying the students driving the cars, searching the cars, and pulling multiple cases together on the students that had enough weed to warrant an arrest. Five more suspensions and arrests were made, and the other three were suspended pending investigation. Another trip to the juvenile center completed their day. Amy, Sean, and Hoss stopped by the precinct at the end of the day to fill out all the reports needed before heading home. It had been a very long day; it was now 7:30 p.m., and everyone was exhausted.

Graduation from the Academy

Thursday morning was a nonstressful, happy day of preparing and practicing for graduation from the academy, which took place at 2:00 p.m. It was a big deal. The officers and their canine counterparts had been through a long, arduous, and difficult journey to get here.

Amy went into the precinct early that morning to complete paperwork and run some leads on a list of individuals she wanted to investigate further. She told Sean she would be at graduation with bells on and was so excited for both Sean and Hoss. She had become close to both of them and considered them very close friends.

Sean picked up his freshly dry-cleaned uniform to change into right before the ceremony. The night before, Hoss had been groomed till his coat had every hair in place and displayed a beautiful shine.

It was the usual walk-through, just like a high school or college graduation, and everyone learned his or her place and what to do. All the officers were beaming with pride and giving their dogs lots of kudos.

At lunchtime, a break was given till two, when the ceremony would begin. Sean went home, showered, had a sandwich, and gave Hoss a couple of treats. He dressed, took Hoss for a nice walk, and then headed back to the academy.

Everyone gathered in place, and the ceremony began. The officers and canine partners were called to the small stage and presented their framed certificates and special badges. The dogs sat during the presentation, and the officers accepted their awards from the head of the academy and then moved on down the line for special congratulations from the chief of police and several of his higher-ranking colleagues.

When all the certificates and badges had been presented, the chief of police went to the podium and added that he had a special recognition he was proud to be part of. He called Sean and Hoss back to the stage. Sean was nervous with pride and completely surprised about this. The chief reviewed for the audience the incident that had taken place while Hoss was in the final stages of training, in which he took down an armed robber. He explained that it was highly unusual during shadow week for a dog to get this type of action on his first day and perform so well. He elaborated, stating that the three robbers were the ones that had been alarming the neighborhood with robberies for some weeks and that this had solved the case and put these hoodlums away. He presented Sean a special gold medallion on a blue ribbon for Hoss. Sean put the ribbon around Hoss's neck, and he looked like a true hero with the gold medallion hanging on his chest. He actually looked as if he was smiling. Photographers and reporters went crazy to get pictures and line up for comments.

The chief then asked Officer Amy Whitehouse to come to the stage. Amy walked toward the podium with trepidation and sorrow. The chief relayed to the audience the rest of the story related to Officer Whitehouse and Chico's leadership in Hoss's training. He gave special commendation to Amy for her bravery, and Amy accepted it with tears in her eyes. In fact, Sean and many others had tears in their eyes. They were all standing there for recognition with their dogs, but Amy was without Chico and would be forever. The photographers again went crazy for pictures. Lots of posing and repositioning for pictures took place.

Afterward, Amy, Sean, and Hoss received lots of congratulations, condolences, and embraces from their fellow officers. Sean and Hoss were targeted for questions and more pictures from the press, while Amy was also asked to pose with them and answer questions. They wanted to know about Sean and his background, Hoss and his background, and what Amy was going to do now without a dog. Sean kept his part short and simply said that Hoss had come to him from God after having been homeless following his owner's arrest. Amy didn't have answers as to what her future held for her, but she was so proud of the time during which she had worked with Chico, who was a well-decorated canine officer.

Sean, Amy, and Hoss left together to find a quieter place. Everyone needed some space with peace and quiet after all that had happened in recent weeks.

A Quiet Celebration

Sean asked Amy if she wanted to join him and Hoss for a short retreat out of Houston. He had wanted to celebrate out of the city, perhaps heading toward Trinity Bay, less than an hour west of Houston. If they were lucky, they would find a cabin, some hiking, and some fun and sun. Sean looked over at Amy, and she was looking at him. He was quick to add, "We would be traveling as just friends; we'll make sure there is plenty of room for sleeping quarters wherever we end up."

Amy smiled and said, "It sounds like great fun; let's go to my place, and I'll grab a small bag." It was the first time he had seen her smile for days. Sean told her to bring only very casual clothes; after all, all their activities would include Hoss.

Hoss could tell that something good, something fun, was in the air as he heard them talking and mentioning his name. His big, bushy tail was wagging left and right; his big brown eyes were looking from Sean to Amy; and his smile was still there, with his tongue hanging out of his mouth off to one side.

It felt so good to take off on short notice, headed for rest and relaxation—and now good company. Sean, Amy, and Hoss seemed so natural together, so comfortable. Sean let Hoss hang his head out the window to get some of the fresh air he so sorely needed. Driving down the highway, Sean was in shorts, shirt, and sandals, looking as proud as a peacock. Amy was in her capris, a T-shirt, and sandals, with her blond hair fluttering back in the breeze from Hoss's window. Hoss was in the back with his nose in the air. They were three cheerful amigos headed for whatever came next.

As they approached San Jacinto State Park, they discussed whether to look for a cabin here or go on across Trinity Bay and pick up something on the beach. They decided to opt for the cabin, as it was more conducive to hiking in the woods, but decided they would take the opportunity to visit the beach over the weekend. They rented a two-bedroom cabin, dropped their stuff and headed to a grocery for supplies. They decided to grill out for dinner, drink wine on the porch, and immerse themselves in nature.

The porch on the cabin went halfway around the house. The prettiest part was outside the kitchen, facing into the woods. Luckily this was the location of the grill, so Sean proceeded to prepare the deck for their feast. The grill was getting hot, Amy was wrapping corncobs in foil, and Sean was marinating some steaks. He had a special surprise for Hoss—a steak of his own, minus the spices. It was the least he could do to show how much he appreciated him. A salad from a ready-made bag was chilling in the refrigerator.

Hoss's nose was busy close to the ground as he ran around the edge of the woods, sniffing out wild smells. Hoss was having a great time already after having been cooped up and made to follow a regimented schedule for weeks. There was something to be said for running free; he remembered it from his past, and there was a sparkle in his eye. Sean and Amy laughed as he sniffed out a rabbit and took off in a wild chase, digging hard to catch his prey. Sean called him back, and he came immediately, dragging his tongue and looking disappointed.

Sean opened a bottle of wine and brought a glass to Amy. He lifted his glass to toast, saying, "To good friends and loved ones." They toasted, looking briefly into each other's eyes, and then returned to dinner preparations. While Sean cooked the steaks, Amy lounged in a chair gazing out at the skyline. The sun was setting low in the distance with a brilliant glow of orange and yellow. She rose from her chair and came over to where Sean was standing. "Thank you, Sean, for being my friend. You and Hoss are so precious to me. I really needed support, and you were there." They hugged as if to finish the thought with closeness. Sean told her he would always be there for her. He added that Hoss was always part of the support, and on hearing his name, Hoss nudged between them for attention. They both stooped to shed affection on Hoss, who at this moment was the happiest dog in the world.

The three of them ate dinner, savoring the food and the moment. Hoss ate meticulously, knowing the steak was all his and no one was going to take it away. He would stop eating occasionally and gaze over at Sean and Amy, who were enjoying the moment.

After dinner, Sean pulled a flashlight from the car, and they took a well-marked trail to walk off dinner. Hoss, feeling his oats, ran up ahead, left, right, and all around. He was walking about four times the distance they were, considering his deviations. They all needed the exercise, and the night air felt good and carried outside aromas. When they returned to the cabin, Amy suggested they just watch television or listen to music for a little while, as she felt exhausted. This was welcome to Sean's ears, as he, too, was feeling the weight of the day. Hoss had already curled up on the rug and was laid out for the night.

Amy and Sean sat on the sofa with another glass of wine, talking about each other. Sean wanted to hear about Amy and her family. Amy wanted to hear about Sean and his background. Both became absorbed in the other's story, each asking questions along the way. Sharing about oneself allows vulnerability, and they both knew that. Police officers always seemed to be guarded about everything—especially sharing personal matters. Once the wine glasses were drained, Amy said goodnight to the boys and retired to her room.

Sean, with Hoss following in his footsteps, went to his room and crashed.

Sean woke early, dressed, and went to make coffee. He found coffee already made and Amy sitting on the porch in a quiet moment. It was that time of day when she loved to have some time alone with her thoughts. She always thanked God for another healthy and productive day. Today she added special thanks for Sean and Hoss's friendship. Sean looked at her through the window for a few minutes before disturbing her. She was very pretty in a natural sort of way, with no makeup, a simple shoulder-length haircut, and beautiful skin. She was fit and looked good in her clothes. She didn't try to "make up" her appearance, even though she was constantly surrounded by men. She was relatively quiet—more observant than quiet, perhaps—and a good listener. She had a strength about her demeanor that was respected. Men never mistook her intentions; this allowed her the safety of being her own person. She had never allowed anyone to take advantage of her either personally or professionally. She pulled her own weight and presented work equal or superior to that of the next person.

Sean joined Amy on the porch with Hoss close behind him. He thanked her for making the coffee and said it was good and strong, the way he liked it. They both laughed and talked about having to get up for the job every day and having time for only one cup of joe. They sat quietly together, taking in the early-morning sounds and smells. Hoss decided to wander down to the edge of the woods to relieve himself and investigate. After a time, Sean said, "I make a mean omelet; what do you think? I love getting a big breakfast on the weekends." Amy told him she could tell by the way he shopped. She got up with him and decided to be the kitchen assistant.

The first thing Sean did was mix Hoss's breakfast; he knew every time he did something for Hoss, it made Amy remember Chico and miss him even more. He felt guilty for it but didn't say anything. Next he chopped up a piece of steak left over from dinner and pulled out some shredded cheddar cheese, salt, and pepper. He asked her about her tolerance for salt and pepper as he whisked the eggs. English muffins lay waiting for the toaster. She decided he didn't need any assistance, so she sat at the counter, facing him as he worked. She smiled and asked him what he was interested in doing today. He began mulling over all the options in the area, but before he could get very far, breakfast was ready. He poured orange juice for them, arranged the omelets and toast on the plates, and said, "Breakfast is served." By then Hoss was lapping up the last of his kibble and looking at the counter, where their breakfast was sitting. Sean laughed and told him he couldn't get too spoiled, as he was a working dog; he could have a steak only when it was deserved. Hoss lay down by Sean's side dutifully.

Amy complimented Sean on his cooking and devoured her omelet just like he did. They both had hardy appetites, and being away from work and near the outdoors seemed to spark them even more. Sean asked Amy what she would like to do, as he was easy about either visiting the beach, seeing the sights, riding through the countryside, or doing anything else she wanted. She said, "Didn't I see fishing rods in your car?" He beamed, agreed to some fishing, and said they would end the day watching the sunset on the beach. He knew a good place for fresh seafood that had a lovely beach and marina.

After breakfast, they packed their swimsuits, towels, and sunscreen along with a small vanity bag containing the necessities of living. He iced down water, beer, and Diet Pepsi—Amy's favorite. He threw some pretzels and nuts in for the road. Hoss was ready to go and somewhat confused about all the fun they were having. He had been through such rigorous behavior training with only rest and food at night for so long that this party was unbelievable. The smile on his face showed a happy camper.

They left for the marina, rented a fishing boat, bought some bait, loaded the boat, and commenced to shove off with Hoss at the helm. Sean verbalized with Amy that he wasn't sure about Hoss's swimming, as they had not spent much time together in recreation. She commented that they would soon find out and did not feel that Hoss would have any trouble adapting to the outing. He barked at the ducks as they motored away from the marina. Sean gave him a stay command just in case he got excited enough to jump into the water after the ducks.

It was the perfect day in the fall of the year, with a crisp air, a sunny sky, and the beauty of autumn colors dotting the landscape. They puttered along for half an hour and found a little cove that looked promising for fishing. He was surprised to see Amy baiting her own hook and casting near the bank as he approached the cove. He cut off the motor, and they drifted for a while before Sean was ready to fish. Hoss was lying in the boat wondering what was next and being extremely obedient and quiet.

Sean and Amy cast for at least twenty minutes without a single serious bite. They decided to move on down the bay to a different spot. As they were moving, a flock of geese came skidding in and landed just ahead of them on the water. Hoss jumped to attention and began a barrage of barking. Sean slowed the boat and told Hoss to jump into the water. He clumsily jumped out of the boat and began swimming toward the geese. They sat and watched the show. He swam as hard as he could with his head out of the water like a kid who had just learned to swim. They enjoyed his fun and could see that there was no way he was going to catch the geese, who swam to shore. Hoss swam to shore, the geese took flight, and Hoss stood shaking off the water and then ran up and down the shore. He was having a great time but was frustrated with the outcome of his assault. Sean motored to shore and dragged Hoss back into the boat. Hoss lay down as if he was exhausted. They continued motoring along till another cove presented itself.

Amy's first cast resulted in a bite. Sean was so excited to get started that he almost capsized the boat trying to get ready. Amy's third cast found a smallmouth bass near the shore, and she fought the fish into the boat. Sean was so proud of her and their catch. Hoss was extremely interested in all the excitement and had his gator eyes big and alert, watching the frenzy. They admired the fish and threw it back into the water. Sean high-fived Amy and praised her fishing ability. They stayed about an hour and a half in this spot, catching six fish, two of which were somewhat sizeable. They threw them all back and decided that they had fulfilled their wish for fishing fun for the day and headed back. As they approached the marina about 1:30 p.m., lots of gulls and ducks filled the area. Hoss went crazy barking, wanting to get into the water. Sean would not allow him to swim inside the marina area and promised him a swim later.

They turned in the boat, gathered their stuff, and took the car down the bay to the beach. They changed into their swimsuits in the restroom and hiked down to the beach with their blanket, their cooler, and, of course, Hoss. Hoss could not believe his luck to be running free at the beach, chasing crabs, birds, and the like up and down the beach to his content. People watched him and smiled; some people stopped to ask about his breed, which was hard to nail. Sean had spread the blanket, rolled up the towels for headrests, and plopped down with Amy to bask in the sun. He pulled out a beer in a Koozie to camouflage the alcohol prohibited on the beach and sucked it down, so thirsty from the morning. Amy had her Diet Pepsi and nibbled on some pretzels. The sun felt so therapeutic to both of them as they lay thinking about the soft heat on their skin as the autumn breeze spread over them like a fan. Hoss occasionally joined them, bringing sand and saltwater to the blanket, which didn't make either one of them happy. But just seeing Hoss have such a wonderful day free of work, free of leash, and free of mind made them very happy. Sean slathered a little sunscreen on his face and nose and asked Amy if she wanted some. Amy took the sunscreen and smoothed it over her lovely skin methodically, gaining Sean's interest.

After an hour or so, Amy got up and gave Sean a dare to race to the beach. They ran wildly to the surf, where they let the water take them in and give them buoyancy. Sean swam toward Amy and tried to grab her. She fled from his grasp, giggling when Hoss joined the chase. She swam out past the first big wave and dared them to follow. Sean followed, but Hoss just circled the area, feeling vulnerability about his capability to catch them. He swam around and around, and Amy smiled to see him just enjoying the water. Sean and Amy connected and then swam to shore. Everyone was panting and running to the blanket. Amy and Sean needed to beat Hoss so as to salvage the blanket from sand and saltwater debris. They dived onto the blanket with Hoss barking— mission accomplished. For the rest of the day, they lazed in the sun and talked about life. Hoss intermittently made beach runs and cleared the area of all birds.

The sun was going down, and Sean had promised to see the sunset. They shivered a little, but bore the lack of direct sun in order to see it set. It was beautiful, and Sean put his arm around Amy, cuddling her in the wind and watching the sun set. Amy looked over at Sean as the sun was setting and kissed him on his ear. Sean returned the intimacy with a soft kiss that exhibited that neither of them had been kissed in a long time. They grabbed their stuff and headed for the restroom, where a quick bath and change of clothes made them presentable for the restaurant.

Instead of putting Hoss in the car, Sean decided to leash him outside the restaurant on the beach and asked for a table for dinner above the girder where he was leashed. Amy and Sean enjoyed a great seafood dinner, occasionally throwing tidbits over the balcony for Hoss. They left happy, full of food and wine. They fetched their comrade, Hoss, and headed toward the cabin.

After eating his dinner, Hoss curled up on the living room rug while Sean and Amy finished off the evening with a bit of conversation.

Amy told Sean that she had seriously been thinking about moving from the canine division to another position. She didn't feel she could deal with training and starting over with another dog—at least not for a while. Sean agreed that she should follow her intuition and perhaps take a break from the division. She would know if and when she was ready for a new dog and could always make that adjustment. She told him she planned to post for an open position in the office doing investigative work. She yawned and said she had experienced a wonderful day thanks to him and Hoss. She kissed Sean on the forehead and said she was going to bed.

Sean went outside with Hoss for a while and walked the immediate area to give Hoss a break before bedtime. He and Hoss sat on the porch for a while. Sean felt he had not been able to pay as much attention to Hoss as normal; it was nice to speak quietly to him and rub his neck. It is true that the endorphins produced in humans when petting a dog give contentment and relax the soul. Sean and Hoss went to bed with a good tired feeling from a pleasant day.

Hoss Makes the Headlines

While they were driving back to Houston, Amy, Sean, and Hoss were sorry their small break had come to an end. It was back to work tomorrow, and it appeared there was change on the horizon for all of them.

Sean stopped for gas at the edge of town and went into the little store to pick up colas. As he opened the door to the store, his eyes picked up the daily headlines. On Sundays, several articles of interest were showcased across the top of the paper, with follow-up stories inside. He moved into the store with his mind playing over what he saw. He stopped inside the door and went back outside, put fifty cents into the hopper, and retrieved a paper. There in black-and-white was a picture of Hoss under the headline "Hero Hoss K-9 in Training." The paper had picked up a human-interest story on Hoss's recognition at graduation. It was a great picture of Hoss wearing his medal, sitting proudly on the police academy stage.

Sean tore into the newspaper, looking for the local news section. There it was! A full page was devoted to Hoss's story. There was a smaller picture of Sean and Hoss together inside the article. Sean ran back to the car to share the news with Amy and Hoss.

Hero Hoss K-9 in Training

Houston's Canine Police Academy graduated a new class of canine officers after eight weeks of intensive training last Friday. At the top of the class was Hoss, who received special recognition for his work during the last week of training, when the canine team shadows another canine team to complete their instruction.

On the first day of Hoss's shadow week, he and his partner, Officer Sean Binkley, brought down one of the three armed suspects allegedly responsible for multiple robberies in the Tusculum area. Two of the three suspects were captured on the day of the robbery, with the third suspect arrested over the weekend. This ends weeks of anxiety and fear in the Tusculum community, as it was the fourth armed robbery in recent weeks in the immediate area.

Hoss's capture of the armed suspect took place several hundred yards from Peerless Pawn Shop, where the robbery was attempted. The suspects fled on foot in three different directions. The first suspect shot and killed a decorated canine, Chico, as he pursued one of the running suspects. Chico's partner, Officer Amy Whitehouse, continued to pursue the armed suspect until she lost him. She returned to the site of the shooting and mournfully found her canine partner dead.

There was a special ceremony for Chico, citing and decorating him for his brave work on the police force. Officer Whitehouse was put on a few days' administrative leave because of her loss. She returned to complete her training of Hoss and Officer Binkley before the week's end.

The Houston Police Department can be proud of its admirable work in fighting crime. Officers put their lives on the line every day when they come to work. The citizens of Houston can tout some of the best police protection in the country.

Tears welled in Amy's eyes as Sean finished reading the article aloud. Both Amy and Sean hugged Hoss and then looked at each other. Sean said, "I don't mind a bit, but the reporter sure tilted the human-interest side of the article to the dog enthusiast. No, I don't mind a bit."

Sean went back to the newspaper stand and bought the rest of the newspapers to send clippings of the article to friends and family. He came back to the car, sighed a little about the excitement, and then hugged

Amy close as he said, "God bless Chico." They drove on to complete their weekend before returning to work on Monday.

Little did any of them know that many of the nation's major newspapers picked up the story and printed it from California to New York. Many supporting and smaller community newspapers also carried the story as it came across the wire to their capital cities and then dispersed to newspapers within their states.

The Boys Hear About It Too

Would anyone have imagined that Charles Witherspoon would pick up the Sunday *Times* in Mississippi and see the picture of Hoss and the exciting article that would cause an anxious stir in his household? He stared at the newspaper after reading the article and then jumped up from the chair to find the rest of the family. It was like finding just what one wanted for Christmas under the tree on Christmas morning and needing to tell someone as soon as possible. It was a candle that had been lit for Grandmother Witherspoon, who had recently passed on to her Lord. Since then, Charles's household had been a sad and sorrowful place. Everyone was trying to deal with Grandmother's loss in his or her own way; she had left them with so much to think about.

Charles rushed into the kitchen calling out, "Douglas, Amanda, you are not going to believe this." He saw everyone in the kitchen looking his way as he burst through the door. He threw the paper onto the kitchen table with the article exposed. Douglas pointed to it as if he couldn't say more. They all looked down, and eyes galore popped with tears, wild looks, and shouts: "It's Hoss! It's Hoss! Where is he, Daddy? Is he alive?"

Everyone gathered around the table while Charles read the article aloud. Douglas and Tiffany's foreheads grew stern and confused as they listened. Everyone began blurting questions. "How did he get to Houston? How did he join the police? What do we do now, Daddy? Can we call him? Can we go get him back today, Daddy?"

While Charles's work truck had been found in Biloxi, stranded and dumped on a side street near the marina, that was all the Witherspoons ever knew. They assumed Hoss had been adopted by the thief or was lost. It had been a sad and unanswered mystery for months now. The family had been dealing first with the loss of Hoss and then with the loss of Grandmother. Charles knew the loss had contributed to her death. She had talked constantly about how Hoss was sent to her as a sign from God that all was well with her precious John in heaven. Hoss was a comfort to her. She had withered away after his loss.

Charles made efforts to calm everyone down, but he, too, was so excited that he could hardly stand it. They all hugged each other and continued talking about seeing him again. Charles requested that everyone let him make the proper contact and find out what he could, and he said he would surely tell them as soon as he knew anything—anything at all.

***

Even more unbelievable was what happened when Ben Brown brought in the paper for his grandpa. They were all getting ready for church—Mom, Trudy Brown, the grandparents, Ben, and his brother. They were in Louisville, Kentucky, temporarily living with their grandparents until their mom saved enough money from her job as waitress for them to have their own place. They had finally been able to get bus tickets to Kentucky from the shelter in Mississippi after the hurricane. They had never heard from their father and he had never called the in-laws to see if Trudy and the boys might be there.

Ben saw a picture of a dog at the top of the paper. He stared in disbelief but then confirmed for himself that it was a picture of Buck, their dog. He ran right past his grandpa to his mom to show her. She said, "Now, Ben, there are a lot of dogs that look like that; that couldn't be Buck. He stayed with your daddy at the mill."

Ben insisted that it was Buck. He said, "No, Mom, there is no other dog in the world with that coloring. Look at the tip of his left ear." It had a tiny nick out of it, just like Buck. He had gotten the injury fighting with another dog.

Ben took the paper to his grandpa to discuss. Ben felt there was no mistaking that the dog in the picture was Buck. Grandpa felt sorry for the kid, who was excited that he may have found a small piece of his past that had been missing. Grandpa patted him on the head and said, "Let's go to church; we'll talk about this later."

The truth is that there was no way Ben could concentrate in church. He may as well have stayed home. He didn't remember a word of the pastor's message and sat with ants in his pants the entire time. Grandfather Scott could see how important this was to Ben and ignored the restlessness in church. He knew he had to do what he could to find out something about this dog to give Ben closure.

Searching for Answers

Monday morning madness at the Houston Police Department began with a barrage of phone calls and emails all related to Hoss.

Schools wanted him to come for visits. Citizens of Houston commended the police department on its active canine unit. Pet enthusiasts wanted to get more information on the dog to share with their clubs and training centers. Dog food companies wanted to interview Hoss for a possible role in a commercial in return for sponsoring all the dog food for the canine unit.

Last, but not least, Charles Witherspoon called to talk with the chief of police about Hoss. Grandfather Davis called to ask who he could talk with about this dog, saying that he belonged to his grandson.

No one was prepared for this—not the police department, not the chief of police, not Houston, and certainly not Sean and Hoss. When Sean and Hoss arrived for work, they picked up on the buzz and looked a bit bewildered. No one knew what to tell the callers; everyone got the standard answer: "We'll take your name and number and get back to you as soon as possible."

Sean's supervisor, Sergeant Koonce, was discussing a new job for Sean and Hoss. He kept being interrupted by police personnel because Sean and Hoss were in his office. Everyone wanted to pull him into this mayhem. He finally got mad and slammed the door shut. Sergeant Koonce smiled at Sean and said, "I'm sure this will die down soon; I wish we could get this type of exposure all the time—you know, the positive stuff."

Sarge went on to discuss the real world with Sean, explaining that it was an isolated and very unusual thing for a canine unit to happen upon a case during the first day of shadow training. He was happy that Hoss came through with all the proper responses; otherwise, they could have been in for a lawsuit instead of all this hoopla. He cautioned Sean to not let this attention go to his head or interfere with his daily duties. After all, Hoss was still a new hire, and it was not yet clear whether or not he would be consistent with making all the right decisions. Work is work and play is play. Now it was time to go to work.

Sarge explained that he would be assigning a permanent beat to Sean and Hoss in the next few days. There were details to be worked out and others to be consulted. Sarge also noted that he needed to speak with Amy and get her plan in place for a new dog—not that it would affect Sean and Hoss. Sean was tight-lipped about Amy, acting as if he knew nothing. He looked over at Hoss, who was lying next to Sean, obediently waiting for what came next. Sarge said, "Do you think it is his good looks or what? He does look like he is smiling all the time with his mouth open and those pearly whites shining." They both laughed, and Hoss looked up at them with his gator eyes, wondering what they were talking about.

Sarge told Sean to go get coffee and hang out in the precinct for a little longer until he'd had a chance to talk with Amy and a few others. Sean headed for the break room, all eyes watching him as he walked. Sean was surprised that the article in the paper had created such a stir. At this point, he had no idea about the phone calls, emails, requests, and offers on the table. He certainly didn't know anything about the two requests that had come through relative to Hoss's past.

Sarge motioned Amy into his office. She continued to get respectful condolences from coworkers who had not seen her since the death of

Chico. Amy put on her business face, went into the office, and closed the door behind her. Amy had known Sarge for a long time—as long as she had been on the force—and had a good working relationship with him.

Sarge said, "You did such a good job with Hoss he has become a hero, it looks like. What do you think of him and Sean?" Amy commented that she had been impressed with Hoss from the beginning and that it appeared he was a valuable addition to the unit. She commended Sean for his work with Hoss and confirmed that he was a good officer.

He asked her if she was ready to train a new dog. Her face fell, and it was obvious she was not. Amy told Sarge that she had thought long and hard about it and would like to post for an inside position, at least for now. He stared at her and asked if she needed more time to think it over. She said no, and he nodded. "You'll have to interview for the position along with others who have posted. I know your credentials are admirable, but what if you do not get chosen?" She acknowledged that she had thought of that and was ready with her answer; she would work in the field as assigned until she found something suitable. She just did not want to work in the canine unit any longer. She unfortunately had gotten too close to her dog and did not want to replace him.

Sarge asked if she would ride with Sean for a couple of weeks until the dust settled, as Sean was still green and could use the contributions of a seasoned professional. He said her previous beat would be a natural slot for Sean if she did not intend to claim it. However, Sarge said he would keep it open for Amy as long as it took for her to train another dog or even if she changed her mind. She smiled and shook his hand as she acknowledged that the plan was a good one. She would go ahead and post for the inside position and ride with Sean for a few weeks. Then they could talk again about her transfer, wherever she was going.

As they stood, he asked her to get Sean so they could confirm the plan. While she was out of the office, the questions began. "Sarge, do we want a dog food sponsor for the unit in exchange for an advertising deal with Hoss?" Sarge looked up as Sean, Hoss, and Amy were coming in and said, "Could I have some privacy, please?"

Sergeant Davis relayed to Sean Amy's plan to post for an inside position but, in the interim, to ride with him to offer added training and information on the beat she had been formerly assigned to. He further noted that this beat would become his permanent assignment—that is, unless Amy ever wanted it back. They all looked at each other, and then Sarge said, "Let's get to work." As Sean and Amy were leaving, Sarge was wishing he didn't have to deal with the distractions this morning. He left his office and said in a loud voice, "Okay, everyone who has a message related to Sean and Hoss, get them over here, and Marge, get me in to see the chief as soon as possible."

Sarge sat at his desk, going over the phone calls. There were eleven calls, and it was only 10:00 a.m. The office outside was still taking calls, and the buzz was all about Hoss. He was going to suggest to the chief that a staff meeting be called to settle things down and get everyone back to work on productive issues. He felt they may even need to have a media conference to put this in its place. And last, but not least, they would have to deal with all the calls and emails. He couldn't forget to meet with Sean and Amy at the end of the day before this got out of hand. Sean would have to deal with this professionally and have all the right answers.

Marge stuck her head in the door and said the chief was ready to see him; she added that he had also called in the department's media director and the assistant chief.

Sarge gathered the messages and started toward the chief's office. Marge handed him six more messages as he passed her desk.

Chief Moran was reading the Sunday article and chuckling. He looked up to see three stern faces and said, "Come on, lighten up; the press is good for us." The only handicap was spending the time on it—time the department didn't have.

The chief pitched an invitation over to Assistant Chief Madison and asked if he could attend the function for him. Madison nodded. The chief then looked at Sarge and said, "Okay, let me have it; let's see what we have here."

Sarge started with the two more serious messages: "We have two different men who say this dog belongs to their families. They want to hear from someone who can talk about the matter. It seems there are kids in each family who are anxious to get their dog back. One is from Kentucky, and the other from Mississippi. "I have nine or ten requests for the dog to make an appearance at their club, school, whatever—some in Houston, mostly everywhere. Oprah and Ellen want to book him on their shows. Two dog food companies want to negotiate deals to use his image on their products in exchange for sponsoring food for the canine unit. Chief, it's only ten thirty; can you imagine what else will come in? Next, Las Vegas will want a six-week contract. I'm telling you, this is hot."

The chief took it all in and asked Joan, the media director, if she thought they should have a press conference to get out some information efficiently as well as squash some of the calls. Joan asked him what information he was thinking about getting out there. He thought about her question and said, "I am not sure; everything I think of sounds wrong when I run it through my head. We have to handle the two potential owners with kid gloves in order not to cause a stink with families, who could play up the tearful children wanting their dog back—that is, if it is true. However, we need them to know that we get our dogs from many different sources, sometimes humane shelters; this sort of thing has come up in the past. Once we take ownership of an animal, put it through rigorous training and put it on the force, it becomes the property of the city. Where did this dog come from?"

Sarge said, "Apparently he was an internal referral from the Biloxi Police Department. The coast guard took him off a fishing boat in the gulf along with his supposed owner. The owner went to jail for outstanding warrants, and the dog was then homeless."

"Did you say 'fishing boat'?" the chief responded. "Who would take a dog on a fishing boat? As for the dog food companies, that's out of the question. We are here to fight crime, not make commercials. And we cannot accept anything free. It is possible, if we want it, to accommodate the television appearances, but only if the story is presented in such a way as to positively impact the Houston Police Department. You know what I mean—a little less attention on the dog, a little more attention on what the department does to fight crime. What do you think, Joan?"

Joan asked, "What about all the other requests for appearances from clubs and schools and such?"

The chief replied, "Perhaps we cannot be selective for fear of retribution from the people. The only thing is, we need to give them all something; this is getting too big to just act as if we are turning a deaf ear to the community's requests. Hell, it's bigger than the community; it's the nation. We'd better get some legal and/or higher-up advice on this one."

Joan offered the suggestion that a news conference be called to respond to the hype on the dog—all in the line of duty. The taxpayer had spent thousands of dollars training this dog for a job—that of a canine police officer whose purpose was to fight crime. The department appreciated the interest in Hoss but had to decline requests for appearances or any media events.

The chief liked the idea of doing this as a general shotgun approach to suppress the phone calls. However, he wanted to personally talk with the two men who called about ownership and also to the show coordinators of Oprah and Ellen. He wanted to smooth out everything as much as possible. Someone in the media department could call all the rest of the people to talk about the news conference, the fact that the police department could not participate in advertising for commercial companies, and whatever else hit the fan.

The chief told Joan to schedule the news conference as soon as possible. He told Sarge to bring the dog and his partner up to speed as soon as possible and to pass all new requests by him, just in case. He made a mental note to meet this dog and at least let his partner know he was a celebrity.

Dear John Phone Calls

"Marge, get Mr. Charles Witherspoon on the phone, but first tell me where the area code is located."

Marge responded, "McHenry, Mississippi ... Mr. Witherspoon, could you please hold the line for Chief Moran, head of the Houston Police Department. Thank you, sir."

"Mr. Witherspoon, this is Chief Moran calling from Houston. The department received your call Monday, and I apologize for the two-day delay in responding. Yes, sir, we do have a dog in our canine unit named Hoss. Well, he just finished his training at the academy and is now working with his partner on the streets of Houston. That would put us in possession of the dog about ten to twelve weeks ago. I see. Yes, he was a homeless animal when we came into contact with him. Actually it was the Biloxi police who offered him to the academy after his supposed owner went to jail. I understand; it is a shame dogs can't talk to us. It would make things a lot easier. Yes, that's correct, Biloxi, Mississippi. Apparently the coast guard was called out to a fishing boat in the gulf where the man who had the dog was seriously ill. The coast guard took the man to the hospital and temporarily fostered the dog. The man's criminal record was run and found to be quite lengthy. He was wanted in several states. Obviously he was going from jail to prison—hence, the homeless dog. I think the man's name was Javier.

"You say you are in McHenry, Mississippi? Let's see; that's not too far from Biloxi, is it? Oh, you are in the cotton business. Ah, so now we know Hoss went with Javier in your stolen truck to the coast, where they boarded a fishing boat. So Javier was one of your workers harvesting cotton. That is a shame. Did you get your truck back? Good.

"You say the dog belonged to your deceased mother? I am sorry, Mr. Witherspoon; losing your mother is not easy. Um, so Hoss was a stray when your mother found him, and she named him Hoss. Yes, the shotgun pellets showed up in his x-rays, but right now they do not seem to be causing him any health issues. Perhaps in old age, arthritis might come into the picture. You don't know how he got shot, do you? Probably an irate farmer. Well, I hope everything is somewhat settled now and the family is okay. Yes, grieving does go on for a very long time. Your son, Douglas—how is he doing? I can understand the bond between a boy and a dog; I had a dog for fourteen years while growing up.

"Well, Mr. Witherspoon, while I can sympathize with your situation, I unfortunately cannot return the dog to you and your son. You understand that the canine police academy gets its dogs from myriad places, including shelters, so the likelihood that many of our dogs had former owners is feasible. The fact is, the Houston taxpayer has spent thousands of dollars training Hoss to become a police officer. He has been given a chance to contribute in a very positive way to society. Thankfully he is very smart and trainable and is already in the midst of his new life of fighting crime. You should be proud of Hoss. He is a very good police officer.

"I'm happy you understand; hopefully Douglas will too—at least in time. No sir, I don't think it is a good idea for Douglas to reunite with Hoss at this point. It might be detrimental to Hoss's mental focus, and I am sure it couldn't be a very happy ending for Douglas either.

"The department does have a file on Hoss, and I will be happy to put these notes of his past life and your contact information in his file, just in case. Thank you, Mr. Witherspoon, for your understanding. If there is anything I can ever do for you, please do not hesitate to call me personally."

Chief Moran sank into his seat after hanging up the phone. This day was not going to be one of his better ones; he disliked the telephone; it was a necessary evil.

"Marge, I've got a blasphemous headache; do you have anything? Do we have any coffee left? Where is Sarge? Did he talk with Officer Sean? Where's Hoss's file?"

Marge rolled her chair to his door and said, "Which question do you want me to answer first?"

Marge placed the phone call. "Is this Mr. Scott?" Hello, Mr. Scott, could you hold please for Chief Moran, chief of police in Houston. He is returning your call. Thank you, Mr. Scott."

"This is Chief Moran from the Houston Police Department calling, Mr. Scott. I understand you called regarding a missing dog? Oh, I apologize; so you are identifying a missing dog. What can I do to help? Yes, I recall that article and picture; it was from our most recent graduation at the canine academy. You say the dog belongs to your grandson Ben? Could you explain a little better why you think this dog is your grandson's? Oh, no sir, this dog's name is Hoss, and he is from Biloxi, Mississippi, not Kentucky. Sorry; I guess I am a little confused. Could you help me understand? Oh, sure, put her on."

"Mr. Chief, this is Trudy—Trudy Brown from Gulfport, Mississippi. Me and my husband and two boys lived there before the hurricane. Our dog, Buck, was left with my husband. I don't know what happened to him. We ain't heard nothing, and we have been scared to death. You see, Jake wouldn't leave, and me and the boys got scared and drove north before the hurricane hit. We are at my parents' house now in Kentucky. We've had that dog since he was a pup. We know it's him, and we want him back. My boys miss him sorely. Yes sir, the way we know he's the one is the dog had a nick out of the top of his left ear from a dog fight, and his swirly colors are perfectly like our Buck. Even his teeth look right; he always looks like he's smilin'.

"Well sir, that would be the day before the hurricane hit the coast. No sir, we ain't heard nothing from Jake; the storm could've swallowed him up. He wasn't too good a man the last few years—the booze and stuff—but he is the boys' father. They are having bad dreams, and we need to know what happened. For sure we want Buck back. He was a good dog—slept with my boy, Ben, and never caused a stink."

"Mrs. Brown, I am sorry for your loss. Thank you for explaining everything to me. Could you please put Mr. Scott back on the line so we can discuss this a little more? No ma'am, it is just that he is the one that called, and I want to communicate with him, please. Thank you, I am sure things will get better. I am glad you and the boys are safe at your parents'.

"Mr. Scott, perhaps we can discuss this a little calmer; it appears Mrs. Brown is quite distraught. Yes sir, I understand; many people are still without a home and have lost a lot during the hurricane. We are still working on many problems here in Houston with misplaced families.

"Mr. Scott, even if this dog happened to be your daughter's Buck, he is now the responsibility of the Houston Police Department. We chose this dog, along with many other homeless animals, to be part of our canine training program. It is very extensive, very expensive, and very important. If the dog successfully completes this program, the next step is to assign a partner and put them on the streets of Houston to fight crime.

"What I am trying to say, Mr. Scott, is that it is not possible to return this dog to your family—even if he truly is the same dog. I hope you can see this and speak with your family about the good that the dog is doing for others. No sir, there is nothing I can do about this. Perhaps you could help the boys get a new pup; it might help them adjust. Yes sir, put her on."

"Mr. Chief, can you help us find out what happened to Jake? Yes sir, I know everything is still a mess; but in your position, I thought maybe you could help. Well, do you know when you can call us back? My boys and me will be up here for a time; I don't have the money yet to get our own place. I heard on the news that the police won't let people go back to the coast yet. Yes sir, I see how much the hurricane tore up the place. Okay, just keep trying, you hear? We'll be waiting to hear from you. His name is Jake Brown, and the address is RR 90, Gulfport, Louisiana. He worked for the Chaswick Lumber Mill there. Yes sir, you too, and don't forget to call us."

"Oh my God, Marge, I need a doctor. All the stuff about this dog is going to kill me; is it worth it? I'll dictate my notes on this to you tomorrow. We could write a book on this one. Take my calls today; I am out of here."

The chief passed Sarge on the way out the door and said, "Sarge, what has Hoss done today—saved the president?"

Sarge looked at the chief and asked if something was wrong. The chief invited him to join him for coffee across the street.

"I'm mentally exhausted from morning phone conversations with the two men who claim Hoss is their dog. That dog has quite a past. Apparently he started out before the hurricane in Gulfport, Mississippi, belonging to a drunk and a low-income family. His name was Buck. He does have a very distinctive appearance, doesn't he? That's how these people are certain he was their dog. Okay, the timing goes that Hurricane Katrina approaches and the family heads north—except for the drunken father and dog. The family loses touch after that with each other. Nothing has been heard from the father.

"I assume the dog survived the hurricane by moving northwest. After some time goes by, he shows up at a cotton plantation, where the woman takes him in and calls him her own. She is the grandmother, and the grandchildren become attached to the dog. Oh, they name him Hoss after the dead grandmother's husband's dog.

"At the end of the cotton harvest, one of the migrant workers takes off with the owner's truck and, of course, the dog. They drive to Biloxi, dump the truck and board a fishing boat in the gulf. Who knows why anyone would allow a dog on a fishing boat?

"The migrant worker, Javier, has an appendectomy attack, and the coast guard comes to their aid and takes Javier and the dog off the boat. One of the coastguardsmen fosters the dog while the alleged owner is recovering. However, this Javier is found to have a record a mile long and goes from the hospital straight to jail.

"The coastguardsman has a friend at the local police department who knows something about the Houston Canine Academy. We'll check this out, but he knows enough to have evaluated the dog to be a good bet for the program. A contact was made, and the dog passed the initial test.

"So in a matter of months, the dog goes from family pet, survives the hurricane and migrates northwest, finds another home, is stolen in a pickup truck, goes fishing in the gulf on a boat, and finally ends up with us. He's been around. No wonder he passed the test; he's a survivor and adaptable to different situations.

"I'll put all the notes in the file tomorrow; I've spoken with the two former owners, and they realize he belongs here now. You might want Officer Sean to review the file at some point, just for posterior. We still have to deal with Oprah's and Ellen's people, the schools and clubs, and God knows what else. Let's hope his activities stay relatively low key for a while. I wouldn't be surprised if the media started following him around.

"I think I'll go get a massage—at the least get my head examined for being such a nice guy."

The Beat

Sean, Amy, and Hoss had been chasing insignificant calls all week. With the influx of individuals and families who ran from the Hurricane combined with the immigrant issues Houston already had, most of the police calls were related to domestic issues, theft, fights, and burglaries. Tent City in Houston had grown tremendously, and the city was working on how to reduce or alleviate Tent City. Sanitary situations were a concern, and the number of fires had increased. The location of Tent City was on the outskirts of Sean's beat in a greenway that followed the railroad.

Most of the burglaries and thefts were occurring at the edge of where Tent City extended into Sean's area. They were minor compared to serious crime, but the retail neighborhood was very concerned. Some store owners who did not have guns decided to get guns to protect their investments. What was now breaking and entering might become more serious.

Sean, Amy, and Hoss were spending the majority of their time patrolling this area and offering police visibility for the neighborhood.

Thursday afternoon they were called to a wooded area near Tent City where someone had stumbled over the dead and mutilated body of a young girl. This was big. Nothing upset the authorities and the community like a murder, especially that of a child. It would be a media fest. Six police cars, including the one used by Sean, Amy, and Hoss, arrived on the scene about 2:15 p.m.

The girl had been dead about two days, and the body was beginning to smell, with flies and small animals having a field day. The young girl was about nine or ten years old. She had been raped and left without clothes with distinct ropelike burns or bruises on her neck, wrists, and ankles.

Her disappearance matched a missing persons report filed that week. She hadn't shown up at home after school. The girl had attended a drama class after school, and the last anyone saw her was around 4:00 p.m., when the kids dispersed. The elementary school was less than a mile from the location where she was found.

Later in the afternoon, a meeting was called at headquarters to discuss the murder; Amy and Sean were asked to be present, as were a number of other police teams. The chief looked none too happy about this meeting, as it now put the city on the spot to not only solve the crime but also do something about Tent City.

The forensics team stated they were already working on DNA at the scene. Matches were being run to turn up anything and everything related to any person of interest who might have been in the area. A team of officers, including Sean and Amy, was tasked to sweep the area with interviews to try to turn up any clue about the girl's appearance in the area or strangers hanging out—any clue at all that might be of help.

Identification of the girl had been acquired, and the family notified. The family had no information to contribute relative to any person or event that would lead to their daughter's death. It was a complete surprise and tragedy to the entire neighborhood. The school and the girl's classmates were in the process of being interviewed.

It was decided that Tent City had to be cleaned up and, hopefully, eliminated. A plan for doing just that began to unfold, with a timeline of three days to implement the tactics. Because all these people were homeless, help agencies had to be ready to receive the people with a plan for their needs. Hospitals needed to be notified of the possible need for assistance. The police department had to be beefed up for the raid and for the interview process of suspects that ended up at the station. This was a complex and delicate maneuver and it had to come off without casualties or humane issues, as the department was under scrutiny to not only do something about the murder but also to show some positive movement in removing areas of concern.

The canine unit was scheduled in full force for the raid. The officers going into Tent City had to be ready to deal with anything. There could be bloodshed. Shady characters with criminal records often find refuge in tent cities and find good camouflage for their comings and goings. Tedious planning was underway.

The Raid

Before daylight, the stage was being set for going into Tent City for a surprise raid. Units were surrounding the area to move in, leaving no escape route. Officers were equipped with bulletproof vests and the normal arms. Sean and Hoss were among the canine units scattered around the perimeter, ready to go. Ambulances lay in wait. Paddy wagons were standing by. The Red Cross had set up a nearby temporary receiving station to deal with whatever came their way. It was decided that all healthy people able to go directly to the stadium were to be processed for placement into shelters.

The mandate was given, and the raid began. As officers entered Tent City, people immediately began to wake up and become alarmed. The ones not in tents jumped up to run. The police, while on the defensive for any violence, displayed an authoritarian but humane demeanor toward the treatment of all individuals. One tent turned up four young girls with older men. The men were armed and dangerous. When the scene presented itself, more police collected at the scene. The men were backed down and handcuffed. The girls looked terrified and did not speak English. The men were quickly taken into custody, and the girls sent over to the Red Cross.

Sean and Hoss were moving through the area when Hoss stopped to sniff a man wrapped up in a blanket on the ground. He was slowly waking up and somewhat dazed. Hoss was very interested in this man, and Sean was surprised that he was acting like this. He quickly pulled Hoss back into position and ordered the man to his feet. The man sluggishly raised to a standing position, all the while trembling with either cold or fear. Sean could see that he had been beaten, as he had visible bruising and a swollen face. He motioned for assistance to get the man to an ambulance. As Sean backed away from the ambulance, Hoss hesitated, and Sean again was baffled as to why he was acting so interested in this man.

Approximately seventy-five people were rousted out and steered into some type of vehicle for transport. One woman was in labor and needed immediate assistance. Two more small children clung to their mother's skirts. The Red Cross assisted with the children as the mother went to the hospital.

The raid took all of three hours, and the remains of the camp were a mixture of trash, fires, tents, clothing, food, lots of liquor bottles, some recreational drugs, and a few pieces of furniture in disrepair. A very unpleasant odor filled the air. The area now had to be searched thoroughly and cleaned up. Investigative units were in place, and the city maintenance workers began their work.

It turned out that the older men who had arms were bringing girls in from Mexico for prostitution. The girls were happily turned over to the Mexican police to be reunited with their families.

The pregnant woman had a healthy baby and was reunited with her two children and given lodging in a local shelter. She was without a husband and needed government assistance to climb the ladder back into society.

Several people who had alcohol problems went to the Salvation Army's program for alcoholics, and many went to the local mission. Their rehabilitation could possibly give them new lives.

Many of the homeless people were ones who migrated up from Louisiana and Mississippi during Katrina. They had no place to go and were struggling to just survive. A lot of work was now being done to make contact with any of their relatives, to place people in a position to be able to work, and, obviously, to meet their immediate needs for clothing and shelter. Most of these people had a sincere desire to either get back home someday or get out of their present homeless situation.

The man who had been beaten and was found wrapped in a blanket on the ground was identified as Jake Brown, the father of Ben and Zack. The chief couldn't have been happier to make the phone call to Trudy to let her know that the sons' father had been found. The family was making plans to drive to town to be reunited with Jake.

Jake's story about his escape from the hurricane with his dog was one of many heard that week from the families who were forced to leave their homes and seek shelter.

Jake was given some medical treatment for his wounds but was now at the stadium awaiting further processing. He was informed about his family coming, and he broke down and cried with trembling hands. A million things raced through his mind, many of which were not good, as he had refused to leave home and felt he had let his family down. His need for a drink, however, consumed the majority of his thoughts, and he wondered if he could even cope with the reunion. He had nothing—no place to go, no way to provide for his family—and he carried a lot of self-pity, anger, and grief. He was a nervous wreck and thought maybe he was going crazy.

Unfortunately the raid did not uncover any clues regarding the young girl's murder. It was decided that the murder investigation was not linked in any way to the people living in Tent City.

Public Relations had done a very good job, moreover, of keeping the public aware of all the positive things the police department had been doing and the goodwill for assisting with Katrina victims, jailing the prostitution ring, and offering general medical and shelter assistance to the general homeless population.

One thing the chief was not looking forward to was the family visiting Mr. Brown, as they had expressed such concern for wanting their dog back. Sean had been counseled about the whole story. Sean then understood the attention Hoss had given Jake Brown. This didn't take away his anxiety over the possibility of losing Hoss.

Anxiety in Houston

Trudy's father was not happy about having to go to Houston to deal with a man who had constantly let his family down and was not a good husband or father. He was not going to let Trudy go on her own, as he didn't trust her to handle the situation maturely. The boys were so excited about the trip—the possibility of seeing Buck—that he could not possibly break their hearts and leave them behind. So plans were made to pack for the trip and drive over to Houston as a family and see what happened.

Grandfather had called the chief and requested permission for the boys to see the dog, and the chief agreed only after confirming with him that the dog would not be going back with them. Grandfather would try to find a way to explain this to the boys on the way.

Sean had talked with the chief and gotten confirmation that the family had no rights on Hoss, and Sean felt better, but he still carried some anxiety about Hoss seeing his former owners.

When word was sent to the stadium for Mr. Brown to be told that the Browns would be in Houston in a few days, Jake could not be found. Jake had given in to panic about the confrontation, along with the overwhelming need for a drink, and he had secretly left the shelter to take care of his needs. He had mixed feelings of guilt and relief as he took his new coat, his blankets, and what food he could put in his clothes and left the building at dusk one evening in search of his continuing life on the streets.

When the chief heard that Jake Brown had left the facility, he knew he had no reason to search Jake out and bring him back. Jake was not a criminal, and if he chose not to receive help or see his family, it was his decision.

By the time the chief called the home, the family had already left and were on the way. Life is full of surprises, and today was no different than yesterday. Why does life have to have so much drama? The chief had seen a lot of things in his career, but this one tugged at his heart.

Good News for Amy

Amy interviewed for a position in the office and was told at five o'clock that the job was hers. She was ecstatic and couldn't wait to tell Sean.

On her way home, her neighbor called and asked her to drop by before going home. Clare had been a good neighbor and had supported Amy during her depression after she lost her dog. She had not spent as much time with Clare and she wanted to since she had met Sean. Now was a good time to tell her the good news and have a little conversation to catch up with each other.

When she walked in, Clare gave her a hug and asked her how she was doing. She could immediately tell that Amy seemed to be in good spirits, and she was anxious to hear what she had to say. They went into the living room; Clare poured a glass of wine, and they commenced to catch up with each other. Clare was so happy to hear that Amy had gotten the job she wanted in the office; she had never been comfortable with her on the streets in such a dangerous job.

After enjoying the wine, Clare said, "You haven't seen the pups since they were born; want to see?" Amy smiled and jumped up to go see the litter of labs. The last time she had seen them, it was hard to tell exactly what they would look like. To her amazement, the mother had nine pups. There were six black and three chocolate puppies.

She sat down on the floor next to the big bed, and all the pups piled out of the basket and into her lap. She was overcome with so much love and was feeling elated with the whole scene.

Clare said, "You know you can have the pick of the litter." Amy just smiled and continued to play with the pups. One of the little black pups aggressively kept trying to get to the top of the heap and get her attention. She started putting the pups back into the basket one by one. As soon as she put the little black one in, she was out again, clawing her way into Amy's lap with lots of kisses and a wagging tail that didn't stop. She laughed and kept putting her back into the basket. It became a game that went on until Amy just picked up the pup and walked into the living room and sat on the couch with it.

Clare said, "It looks like she has chosen you." Amy looked wistful and continued to play with the pup. "They are ready for new homes now; Amy, you need a new friend. You know labs are the best friends you can have."

Amy said, "Okay, you win; I really do want the pup; it will be good for me. Can I pay you?" Clare refused and just reassured her that it was her pleasure to give her the pup as a gift.

Amy said she had to go, as Sean and Hoss were coming over and she had to think about dinner. Clare fixed her up with enough puppy chow and blankets for a bed and smiled as she closed the door behind Amy. She felt so good that Amy had accepted the dog; it would help her depression.

Amy took the puppy home, made a little bed in a box for her, and decided to have Chinese delivered for dinner.

The puppy wouldn't stay in the box and was under Amy's feet every step of the way. She decided to take her outside for a break. The puppy responded, and Amy made a mental note to get a crate tomorrow to start the housebreaking process.

Sean and Hoss arrived, and what a surprise for them to see a new puppy. It was so small compared to Hoss that Hoss didn't quite know what to do with it. After a good sniffing, he decided to just lie down on the rug and ignore it. Amy talked a mile a minute about her day, her new job, her new puppy, and how it had all transpired. Sean was glad to see her happy again.

The Chinese arrived, and they decided to eat in the living room and watch a movie. Much to their surprise, they noticed that the puppy curled into Hoss's middle. Hoss looked embarrassed, got up, and moved to the other side of the room; but the puppy followed, waiting for Hoss to lie down. Amy commented that this was the first day the puppy was without its mother and maybe Hoss was helping with that.

Sean laughed and started to tell her about Jake Brown and the family on the way to Houston. She reassured him that the chief had said there was no way the dog would be given up. Sean said he couldn't help but remember how Hoss had reacted to Jake and wondered if Hoss would want to be with his former family. He would feel bad taking him away from his family. Amy assured him that he was Hoss's family now.

Dolly

Amy worked out a deal with Clare to care for Dolly while she worked. "Dolly" seemed to be the perfect name for such a beautiful animal. She was too young to go to the commercial day care facilities, and this arrangement would be perfect in that she would get daily interaction and comfort from her family. Life couldn't have been better for Dolly; she would be spending days with Mom and the siblings, and nights and weekends with her new mom.

Amy still had the big crate that belonged to Chico. She put a divider in it to make the space smaller for a little puppy and placed a soft, furry dog bed inside with a fleece blanket. Dolly had her own condominium and seemed delighted with it, with one exception. At night she missed the warm body of her mommy, and she whined for hours till she was exhausted and had to go to sleep. This was not a fun time for Amy either, as she was losing sleep and having to go to work; but she fully understood the drill of raising a new puppy.

Dolly was jet black in every way; Amy could not find a white hair anywhere on the dog. One might think that with Labradors being of three colors of varying shades that the colors would be more mixed on the individual dogs. Nature has its way of creating beauty, and it is always in the eye of the beholder.

Dolly was becoming very attached to Hoss, who visited almost every night. Her eyes would glisten when Amy said his name.

On the other hand, Hoss was tolerating Dolly very well. He had been given instructions by Sean not to harm the puppy, and unfortunately for Hoss, this meant allowing the puppy to crawl all over him and tug at him, and best of all for Dolly, to nestle against his belly for a nap.

Sean and Amy spent many hours laughing at the dogs and observing all their shenanigans.

Hoss would lie down in a corner, Dolly would move in and curl against his belly, Hoss would get up and move to the other side of the room, Dolly would look bewildered and move over to him again, and Hoss would finally end up sitting in front of Sean, hoping Dolly would leave him alone. He would also get a stroke from Sean and Amy, which reinforced his spot.

Dolly was becoming more and more socialized with her visitors and her day care friends. She was a sensitive and loving little princess and captured the hearts of all around her.

The Brown Family Comes to Houston

The chief had received a phone call stating that the Browns had arrived in Houston the night before and asking him to call their hotel first thing in the morning. He had been waiting for this message and was dreading the day. When he arrived at the office around eight, the Browns had already called and left another message.

The chief took his coffee and headed to his desk to think about the phone call before talking to the Browns. He knew he had to visit with them not only about Jake Brown's disappearance, but also about Hoss. He checked to see if Sean could swing by his office around ten and wait outside until he was ready for him to come in. He told Sean that he was having the Browns come to his office and had to have a little time with them to talk about Jake Brown. He explained that his intention was to address the dog situation by bringing him into the office and do a wait and see. He ultimate goal, of course, was to stage a parting message for the family about the dog's new life—that is, if Hoss was identified as their former pet. Sean agreed to be in the wings at ten. The chief talked with the grandfather and asked them to come down to the precinct to visit with him.

The Browns were in place within forty-five minutes. The chief was informed that the whole family of Trudy, her parents, and the two boys were present. He anticipated that to be true. He asked for a couple of extra chairs in his office and went to meet the family.

As he approached the family, he saw both hope and worry on their faces. Grandfather stood and shook his hand and introduced the chief to the family. The boys just looked at him, a little bewildered. The chief invited the family back into his office and waited for them to get settled. Everyone looked a little wild-eyed while waiting for the chief to speak.

"I know you have driven a long way to be here, and I have been very excited about the opportunity to reunite you with Mr. Brown. So that you understand all the details surrounding his presence in Houston, I took the liberty of learning from the social workers who have worked with Jake.

"He was among the people in what we called Tent City, a place where homeless individuals collected to live-many of whom had migrated into the city from Hurricane Katrina. Obviously, places like this harbor a lot of not-so-good people who are down and out or have social problems. The area had become a bit of a problem for the city, so a raid was ordered to search the area, assist with the needy, and make any needed corrections to society. Jake was wrapped in a blanket and asleep at the time of the raid. He was redirected to our help center like most of the others. There he received food and clothes, and he was given the opportunity to get assistance with housing, and some direction for the future. While Mr. Brown had no life-threatening medical issues, it was identified that he had a drinking problem that probably contributed to his having sought refuge in a place like Tent City. He was alone and did not appear to have friends or family with him.

"The only reason I was made aware of Mr. Brown as an individual among many was because of my connection to you regarding the dog and your plea, Trudy, to help find your husband."

Trudy interjected into the conversation at this point. "Where is he? Can we see him?"

Her mother took her hand, and the boys began to look worried. Trudy was really nervous and said, "I just want to get on with it; I want to know he is okay."

The chief decidedly answered, "When Mr. Brown learned that his family was on the way to Houston, he walked out of the center and disappeared. He had experienced some anxiety on hearing that you were coming, but he also was relieved to hear his family was safe. He showed a lot of emotion when he heard about you and seemed relieved—just like you felt, most probably, when you heard he was alive. I suspect you knew that he had a drinking problem, and you have to know that anxiety often causes these individuals to make poor decisions with their lives. They do not handle stress well, especially if they are not in a position to make a positive impression."

Trudy started crying, and the boys grabbed closer to her, looking scared. Grandfather asked if there was any way to find him. The chief explained that Mr. Brown was not a criminal and that the police department had no cause to search him out, especially as he didn't want to be found. He could not be considered a missing person, so his disappearance was out of his hands. The chief expressed how sorry he was that the situation did not turn out differently and asked if he could get anyone coffee or water. No one seemed to hear his request. Everyone just sat together looking at each other during a blurry few moments.

Ben looked at the chief and said, "What about Buck? We want to see Buck."

The chief took on a solemn look and attempted to set the stage for a clear understanding of the dog's new life with the Houston Police Department. "Boys, first, we do not know for sure if the dog in question was indeed your pet. We will be able to allow you to see the dog; however, I need for everyone to understand that even if the dog was your pet at one time, he now has a different life—one which cannot be changed.

"Now first let me try to explain all the details. The police department selects many dogs to train and have an opportunity to serve their community in law enforcement. These dogs are not just any dogs; they are very special—at least the ones that are able to go through all the training and pass all the tests to become part of the canine unit are very special. They are smart and have the ability to obey orders, and their lives are then dedicated to doing good.

"Even if this dog was once your pet, he was selected as a homeless animal and became part of a very important operation. It is not often that a dog goes from being a pet to being a police officer; it just so happens that someone took special interest in this animal and pushed to get his nose in the door, so to speak. So, you see, just understand that you will meet this dog; but no matter what the circumstances were before we found him, he is now the property of the police department; he has a new home and a new owner, and he will remain here in Houston with his new owner."

Everyone, especially the boys, sat with open mouths, listening to the chief. This was ending up just like Grandfather had explained; it was not as if they had not heard it before, but there had always been the hope that they would find Buck and take him home. Tears began to flow from Ben's eyes as he timidly said, "Can we see him?"

Trudy spoke up and said, "Now, sir, you listen to me; if that dog is Buck, he belongs to us and needs to be with my boys. My boys have spent many a sleepless night wondering and worrying about their pet, and we didn't come all this way to just visit. We came here to see Jake and to take Buck home."

Grandfather confronted Trudy, stating that she was out of line; he said the Houston Police Department had gone out of their way to work with the family in searching for Jake and had also given the dog an opportunity to have a new home and a new life. "I think we need to calm down and face the music," he said. "It is not like the dog is not being cared for or being abused. We should all be proud that Buck has had such a great opportunity." He looked over at the boys and said, "Now boys, the chief is willing to let us see the dog, but we need to understand that it is what it is now, and we all must move on. Isn't it a much happier thing to find out that Buck is a proud police officer and leading a great life rather than finding out he is dead on the side of the road?"

The boys nodded in affirmation and looked at the chief. Trudy just sat silently in her chair with a defeated and sad look of losing the battle. Trudy's mother reached out to comfort Trudy and the boys.

The chief spoke to his assistant on the intercom and asked that officers Sean and Hoss come into his office. All those present were on the edges of their chairs, and a very long silence fell upon the room and seemed to last a lifetime.

Sean and Hoss entered the room and looked around at the group gawking at them. Sean stood with Hoss at his side while the chief introduced them to the group. Ben gasped and said, "Buck! Come here, Buck." Hoss looked at Ben but didn't move. Ben crossed the room and sat in front of Hoss, reaching out to stroke him. Hoss was gentle about receiving the touch and looked at Ben but didn't move.

Sean said, "It's okay, Hoss, lie down." Hoss lay down on the floor, receiving lots of hugs from Ben. He licked Ben's face but remained in control of himself while at Sean's side.

"That's my Buck, Ben said with a happy and tearful but concerned face. "He looks all grown up and trained to be a police dog." Grandfather called Ben back to his chair, and the chief dismissed Sean and Hoss. As they left, Ben cried while his grandfather instructed him to stand and shake the chief's hand.

Grandfather said, "Chief, we thank you for letting us see Buck, I mean Hoss, and we would like to go now." The chief couldn't say more than "You're welcome." He stood back while the family filed out.

Sean and Hoss moved out of the area to the back of the building, both of them with hearts full of emotional tugs. Sean dropped down and hugged Hoss, almost in tears. It was over. Sean wasn't going to lose his dog. He was thankful and full of sadness at the same time. Seeing that little boy so wrapped up in joy to see the dog had been almost more than he could handle. He was so grateful to Hoss, who handled himself appropriately in his new role as a police dog. The chief came to the back door and called them in. "Okay, men," he said, "let's get back to work." The day proceeded according to schedule.

What About Jake

We always wonder how people can stoop so low as to allow drugs or alcohol to take over their lives, causing them to lose their loved ones and all their possessions just for the sake of a drink or a high. It is a hard thing to understand, but to an addicted person, it happens quite easily.

It may start out somewhat innocently or socially and escalate over a period of time, or it may happen quickly. Whatever the journey, it takes along with it families and friends, causing heartache and pain. It is like a slow death.

Jake's journey started as a young man having inherited addictive genes. As he was part of a family with a low income and had a stressful lifestyle, it was easy for him to try to numb the pain with alcohol. Unfortunately, he was one of those people who grew angry when drinking. He took his frustrations out on his family. So his disappearance during the hurricane was traumatic for his family, but it was also just another bad dream. The Brown family was still internally processing what his disappearance meant to them.

Jake had been living anywhere he could, panhandling by day and drinking by night. He kept to himself mostly, with the exception of a couple of older men, Jerry and Steve, with whom he shared the nights huddled close by for safety. His life's belongings fit into a tattered backpack. The men hid their blankets every morning and hoped they were there to return to at night.

Jake thought about his family often. He still wondered about their well-being but was sure to keep his thoughts as numb as possible; it pained him to think about it. He felt so guilty about so many things—almost everything. He was a failure. He hadn't listened to his son about the danger of the hurricane; he had let his drinking speak for him. He was selfish and had treated his family like second-class citizens, pushing them aside for his own needs. He put them in harm's way, including Buck, who had stayed by his side till the last minute.

Thoughts about these things were debilitating to Jake, and he avoided dealing with the guilt by just drinking till he fell down and blacked out, hoping he could die. Too many days, one of his buddies would have to collect him and get him to a safe place for the night. They knew he was on a road to hell and had begun to look for him by early evening if he didn't show up for the night.

Jake's body was showing signs of alcohol abuse, not getting enough nutrition, living out in the elements, and stressing every day. His family would not have recognized him. However, when awake and moving through his day, he still could show instant anger at the world for the slightest inconvenience—especially if someone showed him any kind of negative body language. And there seemed to be plenty of both around.

A new couple, Perry and Carol, started hanging with the guys at night. They eased in with conversation, bringing a little entertainment and a few laughs. They loved to drink but also were into a few other narcotics. Having a female around was a nice change in one sense; in another, the guys thought it might put a damper on their lifestyle. They trod cautiously with the new people, not causing any problems to run them off. Jake was especially quiet about the new group and preferred to just drink off to the side and try to dull himself to sleep.

After several nights of later-than-usual chatter, Jake was frustrated. He couldn't fall asleep as usual even after finishing his bottle. His head hurt, and the ground felt harder than usual. He got up, grabbed his blanket, and walked out of the camp, throwing out a few choice words about a hard day, respect for sleep, and the noise. The others looked at him wide-eyed and returned his banter, wishing him good riddance.

Jake wandered along the creek, looking for a place to retreat. He felt shaky and confused. He didn't need to stay back there any longer, for he knew he would lash out and cause a real problem; it would be better if he just got out. It was late—too late to link up with others; he could get killed wandering into a camp this late. He cursed the night, he cursed his life, and the crickets responded with their usual song.

He kept walking and looking for safety until he felt sick. He had to stop and empty his stomach. It wasn't the first time he had poured out his guts; he could almost feel the retching coming from the bottommost pit of his stomach; when nothing was left, he coughed up enough blood to make him nauseated again, but there was nothing left. He crawled over to the creek and sank most of his head in the water to stop the retching, to clean the vomit, and to make himself feel better. "Lord, take me now; I'm too much of a coward to take my own life," he muttered. He lay there for hours till the light of morning crept in and he was able to regain the strength to move.

Jake found a shady spot to rest and wait for the morning to progress so he could make his way to the mission. If he was first in line, he could get food and possibly clean clothes. He couldn't think any further than that, dealing with one thing at a time.

Jake

Jerry, one of Jake's buddies, came around looking for him at his usual corner the next day. A few apologetic words were exchanged, and Jake agreed to come back to camp that night. The truth is that he didn't really have anything else in mind; it was an easy choice. He had a belly full of breakfast and enough coins in his pocket to buy a bottle and something to eat for later. He promised himself to start a little later tonight with his drinking; his stomach was still raw from retching, and he thought that if he started later, he might sleep better.

He had all the heat he could take on the corner. He headed to the convenience market and bought his bottle of whiskey plus a miniature bottle that he needed right away to stave off the nerves. He chose a ready-made day-old sandwich on sale. It was dusk, and his buddies were already in place and well on their way. Jake arrived about the same time Perry and Carol came; there was definitely some heavy air from the night before.

Perry settled in against a tree and commented that Jake must have gotten over his antisocial evening. Upon hearing this, a shudder of anger ran along Jake's middle back, and he was about to retaliate when Jerry jumped in and said, "Let it go, Perry; you looking for trouble?"

There was a pregnant pause. Jake added, "I ain't lookin' for trouble, but I ain't running from it either; you have a problem with me, bring it on." Perry looked smug and didn't respond. The group went quiet until Carol started singing a little song and telling a story about a motor vehicle accident that day on their corner. She was sure it had been caused by the boys flirting with her and not paying attention to the car in front of them.

Jake was swigging his bottle pretty rapidly by now, trying to take the sting out of the night. Jerry and Steve had been drinking much earlier, but they had become alert and on guard since the others had come in. All of a sudden, the air was thick with tension.

Perry had undoubtedly been into more drugs that day, as he was definitely on edge and confrontational. He looked at Jake and said he had been aware of Jake staring at Carol's obvious beauty the night before and wanted to make sure he kept his grubby hands to himself.

Jake was aghast, and so was everybody else. Jake never missed a beat. He jumped over the space right on top of Perry, trying to bash his head in with his fists. Everyone stood up and at first didn't know what to do. After a minute or so, they tried to separate the two men. Drunkards do not do a good job fighting each other; nor do they do a proper job of stopping a fight. Therefore, this fiasco went on for a while longer, tearing up the camp with men falling all over each other and Carol getting a hit in on Jake once in a while between whimpers for Perry.

Perry escaped long enough to get a gun from his knapsack. He shot Jake in the head, Jerry in the chest, and Steve in the leg. He was yelling at Carol to collect herself to go. He turned around on his way out of the camp and shot Jake again in the chest and Jerry again in the arm. Perry and Carol commenced to run for their lives.

Someone heard the gunshots and called the police. Three squad cars arrived within minutes, one of which contained Sean and Hoss.

Jake and Jerry were dead, and Steve was hospitalized.

Did God answer Jake's prayer to take him, or was he punished before going to hell?

***

The first responder, Sergeant Collins, gave Sean the report that two men had been found dead from gunshots and one had been found wounded. The wounded one was being collected onto an ambulance and receiving medical attention. He was identified as Steve Harper from his belongings. All of the men were obviously homeless people sheltered in this area for the night.

The area was still being searched, and information collected on the homicides. An alert had been put out to be on the lookout for anyone of interest running from the scene or acting suspicious. Sean and Hoss walked with Collins, who was walking and talking and calling for assistance with fingerprints and investigative personnel. The lighting was poor, so the scene was being taped off to keep the area from being tampered with and the public at bay. As the two dead men were being collected, Sean caught a glimpse of Jake's face and took a double-take. He said, "I think I know this one." Hoss was alerted by sniffing and was seemingly interested in the body. Jake was collected onto an ambulance and sent off to the hospital. Collins produced some ID information that had been collected and said, "Says he is Jake Brown, from Mississippi." A knot formed in Sean's stomach. He knew one part of the puzzle was now solved for those poor little boys; their father was not coming home.

Collins asked if Sean would be willing to take Hoss and search the perimeter of the area—not the creek brush during this darkness, but the street crossings and immediate area—to see if anything turned up. He was to stay in a safe position till dawn, when more officers could canvass the creek area and the brush areas. Sean agreed and took the car to drive around the area, trying to think through what a guilty runner might be doing coming from the scene, and what was in the area that was safe to run to. He noted that the mission was in close proximity to the scene. Otherwise, all was quiet. After a couple of hours, he called in for further instructions. He wondered if he needed to go to the hospital to interview Steve Harper. The chief said they were already on that and asked him to come into the precinct, as it was close to the end of his shift.

Sean was anxious to speak to the chief about Jake Brown. He remembered how the faces of those two little boys had affected him and how scared he had been at the time that Hoss would falter. Truthfully, he would not have blamed him if he had; love is a special bond—one that is not easily forgotten.

Sarge waited for Sean, as he had heard that Sean had identified one of the dead as Jake Brown. Sarge had worked a double, as Houston had been overcome with calls since noon. He was stressed and grouchy and was not happy to hear that the Brown family's troubles had raised their head again. It seemed they had just said goodbye to the family.

Sean found Sarge nodding at his desk, trying to sort through the day's reports. Sean apologized for taking more of his time, knowing that today had been challenging for the police department. He just wanted to see if Sarge had anything in mind for him as it might relate to the follow-up with Jake Brown's death. He stood in the doorway, waiting for Sarge to notice him; Hoss was behind him.

Sarge was startled alert and told Sean to sit down and tell him what was bothering him. Sean commenced to just note the incident, trying to be brief. He expressed that he had concern for the Brown boys after meeting them. He then asked whether there was anything else for him to do. Sarge grumbled that the department would handle the details and told him to go home and get rested for a busy shift tomorrow.

Sean was a little surprised at Sarge's comments, but he nodded and got up to leave and go home. He felt heavy, as if he were carrying around a weight, though he wasn't sure why. He figured he was just tired, and he took his buddy and went home.

He showered and went straight to bed after feeding Hoss and taking him on a short walk to let him do his business. These odd hours didn't agree with his body; he figured his body rhythm was off and that rest would be good.

Rest didn't come, though. He tossed and turned, though he did fall asleep for a while, dreaming about Hoss as Buck playing with the boys and living with the Brown family. Buck was so happy, and the boys slept with their best friend every night. He woke suddenly with a jerk to see Hoss lying on the rug close by. He was drenched in sweat, and his heart was beating wildly. He thought maybe he had had a panic attack or something. After a few minutes, he figured out that it had been a dream.

His mind was racing with all kinds of questions. He knew why he was having anxiety. His heart was full from thinking about those boys. They had gone through a major hurricane, lost their home and all their belongings, and were basically homeless with a somewhat weak mother for a long time. *What kind of trauma is that—wondering what happened to their home?* They had lost their father and their best friend, their dog, which were major events. Thank goodness there were grandparents for them to finally fall back on.

Now they were going to hear that their father was dead—never coming back. They'd already heard that though their dog was out there, he was never coming back either.

Sean knew he had to move all this out of his head. He was trained as a policeman, and he knew these were precisely the types of things policemen see and deal with on a day-to-day basis. He had been trained not to take it home, but to do the job and separate himself from the emotional parts.

Needless to say, the next few days were tough. He found it difficult to overcome fatigue and tough to try to normalize his emotions. He learned Sarge had called Grandfather and requested that he or Trudy come to identify Jake's body and make whatever arrangements they wished. Sarge did not share with him any of the details. Sean knew not to ask.

Sean had many nights of dealing with his anxieties and trying to work through what was going to be the right thing to do for him to shake the guilt of having Hoss. He felt he had to do something to counter all this for the good. He wanted to help make it better and to help the boys move on with their lives on a positive note. He wasn't there yet, but he knew Hoss was the key component. He also knew his job could be on the line if he were to show weakness or emotion. He asked God to help him sort it out. He asked for help. He loved Hoss with all his being and was ready for Hoss to also help with that decision. He hugged him close and prayed that God would give them an answer.

Putting Jake to Rest

Grandfather took the call from Sarge informing him that Jake had died. He gave surface details of the homeless environment, the unsolved crime of the shooting, and that Jake's body needed final identification and arrangements by the family. He of course delivered the message with his sincere condolences and offered any assistance as needed. He gave all the pertinent information to Grandfather and hung up the phone. He immediately left for lunch and took extra time to take a long walk through the park. *Yes, we are all policemen,* he thought, *but sometimes there are a few things that just tug at the heart.*

Grandfather was numb after the phone call. He knew he had to give the family some very bad news that would make a major impact on their lives. He had to think just a while how to do that and make a plan. He and Grandmother spent hours that night talking about it. It was decided that the best thing to do was to just bring everyone together and give them the news of Jake's death. They wrestled over whether or not to talk about a gunshot wound—a homicide—thinking perhaps it might be better to deliver a message about poor health from drinking. It would be less traumatic for the boys. But for Trudy, who would want to go to Houston, she would have to know. It was Friday night, so Saturday morning would be the family meeting. They braced for the worst, not knowing how Trudy or the boys would react to the news. They knew, though, that this would be a puzzle piece they had been waiting for to gain closure with all the tragedy.

The family awoke all within an hour or two of nine o'clock, and Grandmother was cooking a nice breakfast. Grandfather was reading the newspaper. The boys turned on the TV for cartoons, and Trudy appeared, looking for coffee. They all enjoyed breakfast. Toward the end, as Grandmother began to gather dishes, Grandfather said there was a family meeting this morning and asked them to gather in the living room.

Grandfather turned off the TV, and everyone looked to him for the next move. Grandfather thankfully had a good bedside manner and a calm delivery when speaking. Everyone always felt comfortable and easy with him; he was the kind of person one just felt comfortable with. He was trying hard to be calm and deliver his message with care but with an important manner so that everyone knew how deeply he personally felt about what he was saying.

Grandfather told them he had important information. He had received a phone call from the sergeant they had met in Houston and had learned that Jake had been found dead, apparently from his drinking. He had been taken to the hospital. Trudy broke down in sobs and grabbed her sons close to her breast. Both of the boys looked traumatized and began to cry. Grandmother joined the scene to console them. Grandfather continued to say that he was in a good place and that God was waiting for him to come over the rainbow bridge to be in heaven. He went on to say, talking along with the sobbing and crying in the background, that Jake had problems that he could not solve with his drinking and that he had asked God to help him. God had decided to bring him to heaven and cleanse his soul and make him a happy angel. "Please remember that your dad is in a happy place," he said.

Ben got into Grandfather's lap and nestled into his body, needing all the love and warmth Grandfather could give. He asked if his dad knew they were okay. Grandfather assured him that he did. "He knew you boys and Trudy were with us, and he felt good about it. He was not ready to get well, so he stayed in Houston. He kept drinking, and then he asked

God to take him and make him a better man. All is well now, boys. Your father is not suffering now."

Trudy asked about his burial. Grandfather said that he felt the best thing was for him and Trudy to go to Houston to make all the arrangements. It was too complicated for the whole family to go. They made arrangements for a flight early the next morning and commenced to make plans to leave. The house remained quiet that day, with the boys staying close to Trudy and asking a lot of questions she could not answer. She promised to be gone only a short time and to stay in touch. She would have more to tell them when she returned. That seemed to help soothe the boys' wounds for the moment.

Grandfather got the pertinent information from the police department, made a hotel reservation for one night, and was able to get an afternoon appointment with Sarge. The plan was to get into Houston before noon, get to the morgue, identify the body, and then meet with Sarge. They would probably need to stay two nights, as some type of arrangements would need to be made for the body. He would be lying if he said he wasn't nervous about this. The hurricane had taken its toll on Trudy and the boys; now there was this tragedy of losing Jake. His family continued to struggle. He needed desperately to move everyone to some semblance of normalcy for their mental well-being.

Trudy had never flown before and was a little nervous about that along with what she was dealing with in preparation for today's business. She was thankful for her father, who had always been a rock in her life. She felt it was too bad she had not always listened to his wisdom. Her years with Jake had not been what she had expected, and she was ashamed and frightened to admit this to anyone. She was not sorry about her boys, however; they gave her purpose and unconditional love. Her father's presence gave her strength; she felt stronger by his side. She knew he would help guide her through this.

They grabbed a cab and went straight to the morgue from the airport. As they waited for the technician to show them inside, Grandfather shared that he could probably do this alone if Trudy felt she would rather not. Trudy said she needed to see him—that she needed to be strong. They went inside, and the shelf was pulled out and Jake's face uncovered.

As he had been shot in the head, it was not a pretty sight. Trudy gasped and backed up as Grandfather kept a close hold on her. The technician asked if they could identify him, and Trudy said, "Yes, it is my husband, Jake." The technician showed them to a break room.

Trudy was so traumatized that she couldn't cry. She felt frozen till Grandfather took her in his arms and said, "It is going to be okay, Trudy, I promise. Jake is in a better place; he is no longer struggling with his demons. I know he loved you and the boys."

Trudy fell apart then and let the tears flow. She cried till she was dry. Grandfather looked stressed and exhausted when he released her and sat back into a chair. They both took deep breaths and decided to have a cola. The technician came to tell them that Sarge had sent a car for them.

The meeting with Sarge did not last long. They were told that the scene was a homeless camp and that some type of altercation took place with shots fired, leaving two dead and one wounded. Investigation with the wounded victim had given them positive identification of a suspect that was on the run. They would be able to find the responsible person and put him away. Sarge expressed his deep condolences for the family's loss and asked if there was anything he could do. Grandfather shook his head and noted that they had to make arrangements for the cremation of Jake's body and wondered if Sarge had a recommendation. Sarge nodded and asked if they were staying overnight. Grandfather said they had a late check-in at the Best Western nearby. Sarge suggested they get dinner and rest tonight and said he would have a social worker call them by 10:00 a.m. tomorrow to assist with their needs. They shook hands, and Sarge said a car was waiting to take them to the Best Western. He also recommended a decent meat-and-three restaurant next door to the hotel for dinner.

Trudy stood at the front desk with Grandpa and said, "Dad, I don't want to be alone tonight; would you mind if we stayed in the same room?" She looked at the clerk, and the clerk said she had a double double if they would prefer. Grandfather said fine; he felt they might need it for two nights, as they weren't sure about their business tomorrow and their flight schedules.

The clerk replied, "No problem. Let me know if your plans change." Off they went to finally get some rest and communicate with the family.

That night Trudy thought about how fortunate she was to have parents who were strong and who loved her unconditionally. Jake had been an orphan; he never knew his parents and never wanted to. He felt deep pain from the mystery. He entered a trade school at eighteen and was on his own from that point on. Alcohol had become his only friend—his only solace. Grandfather was right; he was in a better place, free now of his demons. She had honestly thought he loved her, and he might have—briefly. She felt so empty. Her mind was racing with bygone memories—memories of Jake when she met him, when he smiled, when he kissed her. She was worried now. She was alone. She wasn't sure if she could do it alone with two boys.

And so it happened. Grandfather and Trudy identified the body, had Jake cremated, and had his ashes put into a beautiful keepsake jar which would be delivered to them in a few days. Grandfather and Trudy enjoyed the bonding of being together and the opportunity to talk privately about so many things that had happened over the years: time that had gone by without contact, time during which the family felt estranged—time wasted. Grandfather knew that this marriage had damaged Trudy and that some time would need to pass and work would need to be done to repair her heart and her self-esteem. He felt at peace that he had his family together and that he could participate as a parent.

Blessed Be the Grandfather

Thank the Lord this family had Grandfather, a strong man who could handle a situation like this, mentor his family, and work through a very emotional time. It was bad enough that Trudy and the boys had had to leave their home, but for them to also have to deal with the loss of Jake and the dog was devastating. In Grandfather's heart, he knew that they were better off without Jake, as he had chosen alcohol over his family. The sadness of the disease was almost too much to comprehend.

He and Trudy came home and knew they were on a new slate, starting over. Thankfully some good discussions had taken place, and also there had been time for some consoling and some understanding between the two of them that all was okay.

The trip home was exhausting, as the flight was in the afternoon; and after a lot of waiting, they collapsed in their seats. It was late when they arrived home, and after a snack and short conversation, everyone went to bed. Grandfather and Grandmother took tea to bed and engaged in some conversation before falling asleep. They knew Trudy was not capable enough to be on her own with the boys. She had no real work skills to properly make a home for them. She was not a strong woman;

she had always been subordinate and submissive and didn't have the proper leadership skills to raise the boys on her own. They decided to move along with caring for the family and getting them adjusted to some kind of normal routine and family life. The boys needed Grandfather to help them grow and feel properly cared for. Trudy needed to find some type of work that interested her to build her self-esteem.

Sleep came quickly, but with the many things on their minds, they were up early and beginning to make plans for stabilizing the household.

After breakfast, Grandfather called everyone into the living room for a family conference. He said that he and Grandmother wanted the family to stay with them—not just temporarily, but forever. He delivered love and comfort to the family by allowing them to know that not only were they really wanted to be one big family, but also that it was a good arrangement in which everyone could feel comfortable and loved. All family members would have jobs of sorts. Trudy would think about what she might want to do and have fun with, and then she could find a proper job to be productive and establish her individuality. The boys would go to school, play sports or take part in extracurricular activities, and make new friends. Trudy, Zack, and Ben all sat quietly with wide eyes, and a good, warm feeling of relief came over them.

The boys started asking a million questions, all of which Grandfather could not immediately answer. He just said, "There are things to be done; we need to move on. First Grandmother needs to visit school with Trudy and the boys and get signed up. Then shopping is in order. We want our boys to look sharp and handsome going to school. I will work with Trudy on her new life. We will make this a proper home for all of us and make room for a new doggie." Everyone's eyes got big, and joy flowed through the room. Grandfather and Grandmother were showered with hugs and kisses, and Trudy sat quietly with a smile, watching the whole thing. For once in a long time, she felt comfort and security. How long had it been since she felt this good?

Giving Back?

On his next shift, Sean asked Sarge how he felt about him getting with the Brown boys' grandfather to see if it was all right for him to get the boys a new doggie. He explained about his thoughts lately and felt that reaching out might help with closure on such an emotional family disaster.

Sarge scratched his head and told Sean to sit down for a few minutes. He said that Sean needed to understand, and he was sure he did, that getting personally involved with cases was a no-no.

Sean nodded and said he knew that, but for some reason, probably because of Hoss, he couldn't stop the thoughts from causing him sleepless nights and feelings of guilt for having Hoss. He knew that Hoss belonged to the police department and was assigned to only him, but he added that as attached as he was to him, he was willing to give him up to the boys if that was possible.

Sarge's eyes grew wide with surprise. He confirmed that Hoss belonged to the Police Department and had become a very valuable asset to the force. The dog obviously was very intelligent, could be highly trained, and loved working. He told Sean that it would be a disservice to the dog to change his life again, as he could never be happy with just the job of being a pet; he needed a real job. He was a different dog now and had made that decision when he met the boys that day in the office.

Sean almost teared up. He had known that. He rose from his chair.

Sarge told him to sit back down and said, "Since I've been the contact with Grandfather, I'll give him a call and feel him out about the boys getting another dog and whether it should be a puppy or an adult dog. You never know, they may not want a dog in their new home or be able to have the right place for one. Let me do that, and I'll get back to you." Sarge gave a sigh, hoping to soon be done with the Brown case. The whole thing had taken its toll on the department, starting with the dog and all the incidents since he had joined them. It was a complicated roll of events, and not one to easily put aside.

Sarge called Grandfather later in the day, though he hated to do it; he knew he would also have to tell him they had not received any more leads on the guy who murdered Jake. He would have to ask about the family and do the normal gracious shakedown besides talking about the dog. He just wanted to offer the services of Sean to help them find a nice dog that would fit the specifications the family might have in mind, as an extended kind gesture.

Grandfather was surprised to hear from Sarge, and he got the updates he wanted on the case. He told Sarge that they'd had a family conference and decided to keep the family together in their home, and that included a new dog. He said the boys had been very happy to hear this, but nothing had been done as of yet. He thought maybe he should discuss this with the family and get back to Sarge.

After Grandfather hung up the phone, he called Sarge back and told him that on second thought, he was making a decision that the boys would choose their own new dog in due time. He felt it might be better for them to bond right from the start by going through the hunt for a new pet and then making a final selection. It would be a great new job for the boys as part of taking on some of the responsibility for the new pet. Sarge agreed with him, and they ended their conversation.

When Sarge told Sean, even Sean understood. He realized he'd been being a bit selfish to think that his involvement would make a difference.

he had been wanting to get involved for himself, not for them. He needed to move on.

As Sean turned to leave, Sarge called him back. He told him he would be a very busy person starting tomorrow morning. The department's media personnel and legal counsel had set up a meeting to go over all the community and national requests that had come in relative to Hoss's heroism. They were ready now to book appearances and stage some very good press for the department and its canine unit.

Sean's mouth was wide open with a grin. Sarge said, "Yes, we'll be seeing you on *Oprah* and *Ellen*, to schools across the nation, to appear in documentaries, and who knows what else. Sean, you and Hoss are now celebrities. Now, if you'll excuse me, I have a headache."

Author's Notes

I am, without a doubt, a dog enthusiast. Not only am I highly interested in dogs, but I spend a large part of my life directly or indirectly involved in various activities related to the welfare and happiness of our furry friends. I'm a sucker for helping the needy.

I presently have a sixteen-year old Labrador mix that was adopted from the shelter at seven weeks. She has been through a lot with me over the last sixteen years; she knows when I'm happy and when I'm sad. I love her more than life itself, and I know her life is very limited at this point. I also have an adopted mutt who broke my heart by sitting at my glass back door every night with dreamy eyes. His DNA turned out to be 50 percent mutt and 50 percent mixed mutt. He is a great dog. I am presently fostering a kitty abducted from a Texas hoarding incident this year; over two hundred cats were rescued, and seventy-nine of those were sent to Nashville, Tennessee, for handling through our NHA foster program.

But there is another dog that sent me on many adventures and inspired me to write this book. His former life before I found him was a mystery to me, because he was a Katrina rescue. If only he could have talked to me. I can tell you his true story, but I had to make up his past—thus the book.

Everywhere I have lived, I have always been involved with animal shelters, pet therapy, foster care, dog walking, kennel cleaning, animal behavior education, dog training, and, of course, lots of reading, even though I work full-time in a totally different field.

My husband, a civil engineer with the corps, was called to work with FEMA right after Hurricane Katrina hit. After a couple of months, I received a phone call from the FEMA office in Wiggins, Mississippi, asking me to please come down from Nashville to check out a particular dog that was hanging out at the office. It turned out that the office had sort of adopted him, letting him in every day and feeding him. He would sleep on the outside door mat at night, waiting for personnel to arrive each morning.

This dog was one of hundreds of dogs in that little town hovering in the dead-end streets and everywhere they could collect for safety. Wiggins was just north of Louisiana, where the worst of the hurricane had hit. People left their dogs or dogs got lost and headed north to escape the storm. The city had begun to be concerned and round up as many of the animals as they could. Shelters all over the country were taking in the sick, wounded, and homeless. But this dog had reached out to make friends; he seemed different. He was a calm animal that appreciated any kindness. The engineers befriended him for that reason and wanted to save him.

I flew to Mississippi; my husband picked me up late at night. We drove straight to the office. The dog was sleeping on the doormat in a light, misty rain. I almost cried as we collected him into the car to take him to the house my husband was renting.

The dog was amazing; it seemed as if he knew we were helping him. He just went along with everything we did. We stopped for dog food, and then went straight home. A closer view of the dog showed he had gunshot wounds in his back that were trying to heal. I drew a warm bath in the tub and gently shampooed him. I carefully blow-dried his fur until it was almost dry. We fed him a little and then walked outside. I had a leash from the shelter—the kind that slips onto the neck—but he didn't seem to want to run away.

I took him to the vet the next morning. She said the gunshot pellets would just need to stay below his skin; she treated each spot with antiseptic. She thought he was about two and a half years old. She recommended he be neutered right away. He got his vaccines. Then she told me he was very full of heartworms; she even wondered if he would be able to go through heartworm treatment. The treatment was a long one—nearly six months—and involved very painful routine shots. He had to remain contained and calm during this time.

We decided to give him a couple of days to recover from his vaccines and feel strong, and then he would come in to be neutered. After the neutering, I decided to take him home to Nashville. I rented a car, and we left; this was the beginning of Wiggins's new life. Wiggins was his new name, as I had found him in Wiggins.

Long story short, Wiggins did great with his heartworm treatment. Yes, it was sad to have to see him endure those painful shots and my heart went out to him when I had to leave him at home to go to work. He was able to go out through a doggie door in the garage into a fenced-in backyard. He was safe.

I had adopted my Labrador, and she was still a puppy, so she was being dropped off at day care every day. She and Wiggins bonded quickly. Everything we did, we did together: our walks, our swims in the lake, our family visits—everything. We even went to a doggie christening.

I wrote a children's book about Wiggins, and we made some contacts in Wiggins, Mississippi, to go back and do book signings, visit the school, and tell Wiggins's story. The mayor even invited us to walk first in the parade that weekend; he was proud to have this little bit of history from his town, and a book and a dog named Wiggins.

It was a grand weekend signing books, having lunch with the mayor, and walking in the parade, and I made several very nice friends in the community. Over lunch I asked the mayor about his animal shelter, as my past history with shelters is always of interest. He changed the subject and said I wouldn't be interested in this. Well, of course, this only piqued my interest more.

I was surprised to learn that no one I asked knew about the shelter or its whereabouts. It seemed as if it didn't exist. I finally found an old man at the local grocery who knew about it, but he acted as if it were some kind of secret or something. I was able to smooth talk him enough to learn it was a good thing that I was here to help. He made me promise not to tell anyone he had told me where its location was. I did, and I promptly drove to the designated location a few miles out of town.

It was not a shelter—just a small fenced-in space. There were five adult dogs, one of which was a mother with six nursing puppies. The dogs were all very skittish, and a couple were sick looking. There was a pretty rough-looking guy there filling up water bowls.

I leisurely walked up after parking nearby. I acted friendly, as though I was just looking around. The guy was chatty enough. I asked about cats. He said they shot the cats because they multiplied and became too much of a nuisance. I looked at the animals and wished him a good day and left. I headed straight for the mayor's office.

Thankfully, this was a small town—probably three square blocks of business buildings with the outskirts of historic buildings and homes, and then farms. One could just walk into the mayor's office and see him if he happened to be there—which he was when I arrived. I told him what I had seen, and I told him what I had heard about the cats. I let him know the whole thing was inhumane. I understood why he hadn't wanted to talk about it. I asked him to make it right. Those animals needed medicine and care, and he was to blame for housing them without caring properly for them. The puppies might live, but the mama dog probably wouldn't. They were all out in the elements, with no protection from the heat or cold. He looked at me and asked me what I thought he should do; he said there was no money for building animal hospitals. I countered that he could be a hero if he did fundraising or something to make a project out of this. He was obviously annoyed with me. He looked at me and told me it would be best if I just left well enough alone and moved on. I left the office. I knew it was now or never; I had to get those dogs out of there.

I headed to the TV station and convinced them to meet me at the so-called shelter site for a live interview for the evening news. I exposed to the community what their animal shelter looked like and what the animals looked like, and I didn't leave out the comment made to me about shooting the cats.

I knew I was in trouble at this point. I called the Gulf Point Animal Shelter on the coast and explained that I had four to five dogs that needed a place to come. They told me they would be ready the next day for me when I brought the animals down to Gulfport. I had to get this plan down, as well as one to further the work toward the overall problem in the city. After stealing the dogs from the so-called shelter and taking them to Gulfport, I needed to have a plan in place for the future.

One of the ladies I had met at the parade and who had been kind enough to let me stay in her little cabin helped me call together a group of ladies to meet about the issues at hand and to help develop a community effort to further the cause of getting a proper shelter in Wiggins, Mississippi. We met, and there was not only great enthusiasm to help me with my immediate issue but also great motivation for moving toward future planning. These ladies were the movers and shakers of the community. I shared my plan to go to the so-called shelter and abduct the dogs early the next morning with the ladies.

It happened like clockwork but with much anxiety. One of the ladies offered to take the mother dog with her puppies to foster, which was a major relief. The other dogs were loaded into my van, and off I went on the road, headed to Gulfport. I started driving toward the coast. It was a forty-five-minute drive to the shelter, but I knew it would seem like forever. I set my head right so that all the commotion of five dogs in my van did not interfere or distract me. For the most part, they were frightened and restless; it could have been much worse, so I was thankful. I called when I arrived, and two attendants came out to help with the dogs.

I had to stay for an hour or two to do paperwork. During that time, I was able to learn that two of the dogs would have to be put down because of health issues. It was a very sad day for me for the most part, but I also felt somewhat accomplished in knowing that maybe—just maybe—the other dogs and puppies would be saved.

I learned that one dog had emptied his bowels in my van, so I had to get over to a car wash and do the best I could to clean it out. Of course, those poor doggies had been terrified. I hoped they were calmer by now.

That evening, I so appreciated my friend caring for Wiggins in my absence, and I began to feel a sense of camaraderie for a cause we had discovered that badly needed attention. We talked for hours about the past and how the community could have been so blind, and then we talked about what to do. It would be a tall order, a very big job, and a huge challenge to work toward, but it would be so worth it to have a proper shelter. In the meantime, with the press the mayor had gotten for the coverup in the community, they were sure some improvements could be made for temporary relief.

I left Wiggins, Mississippi, with Wiggins, knowing I could not do more; it was up to the community to do the job. I resumed my normal life and continued on until one day about three years later.

I was walking my two dogs in Santa Cruz, California, one sunny day when a call came through to my cell. It was the woman who had fostered the mama dog with the puppies six years earlier in Wiggins, Mississippi. She said, "Is this Shirlee Verploegen? I want you to know that we now have a proper animal shelter here in Wiggins, and it wouldn't have been possible if not for your dog, Wiggins; we have painted his picture on the wall of our entrance."

I was so surprised, happy, and elated that I fell to my knees and pulled both my dogs, Wiggins and Dolly, to my breast and cried tears of joy. Sometimes the seeds of actions planted by doing the right thing in your heart for the sake of a life might blossom into a beautiful flower and touch more hearts and save more lives. Always do the right thing.

Note the hard work of Katie Stonnington, director of the Stone County SPCA (ktstnn@aol.com), as well as that of her committee workers. "Animals began being fostered in February 2010. As of 12-28-2011, the group has taken in 485 animals. These animals have been adopted out or transported to shelters in need of animals. Kate Stonnington reported that "no animals have been euthanized due to overpopulation."

REFERENCES

Wilson, Charles Reagan. *Chinese in Mississippi: An Ethnic People in a Biracial Society.* Mississippi Historical Society.

The Truth About the Boll Weevil. Mississippi History Now.

ThatMutt.com ... a dog blog. Sound Off Signal Publication Online.

Criminal Justice School Information-Police K9-Unit Training Online Publication

Free Preview

Buck, Jake, and Floodwater

Finally, after the worst of the storm, Jake and Buck left the building in ankle-deep water. Less than ten minutes later, the streets were gushing with floodwater deeper than they could stand up in. The current carried them along, gasping for air and looking for something to grab onto.

Buck and Jake could swim, but they floundered in the water like rag dolls. Buck was traumatized and kept looking around for his master as he was carried along in the water. Jake had grabbed onto a tree and was hanging on for dear life. He watched Buck go downstream with the current, unable to do anything about it. Jake was weak and hysterical as he clung with all his strength to the tree and wondered for the first time about his family. His dog was gone, and now he was all alone.

Jake hung on for about four hours before someone in a boat came along and tried to pull him from the water. In trying to get him aboard, the boat capsized and all three men fell into the water. They managed to grab the boat, haul themselves back inside, and finally get Jake inside as well. Jake was sick, cold, weak, and exhausted. They moved on to get some medical assistance for Jake and continue watching for other flood victims. Jake lay dazed in the boat, shivering and somewhat delirious.

Buck swam among the rushing water and was swept along by the current for a long time until he found a piece of wood to pull himself onto. He was exhausted and coughed up a lot of water. Buck tried to keep his balance on the piece of wood for as long as he could. I am sure it was hours, but for Buck it seemed like a lifetime. He traveled at least five or six miles down the flood creek and finally came to a patch of higher ground that the wood ran aground upon. At this point, Buck and his wobbly legs came ashore, and he wondered what to do next. All he could do at the moment was lie down, rest, and try to regain his strength.

Jake was taken to a local and temporary medical facility, checked over, and allowed to rest until his strength came back. He was fed bread and jam, water, and dried fruit, and he seemed to feel a little stronger within a few hours. The problem was that his need for alcohol was kicking in with a vengeance, and he had stomach cramps, nausea, and almost hallucinatory thoughts of bugs and other unpleasant things crawling on him. He was experiencing delirium tremens, or DTs; people with alcohol dependency are all familiar with these symptoms.

He remained in the medical area and had to deal with this without much attention to his needs. There were too many other people who were missing or had been rescued with life-threatening issues for medical personnel to give Jake enough time to sort through his personal problems. He moved from the medical facility to a local shelter and began to get sicker, not only because of his physical issues but also because of his mental ones stemming from his having ignored his family. There was no power and no functional phone lines. The Brown family didn't have a phone at the house, so it was doubly frustrating. Everyone was talking about the devastation, the deaths, the floods, people stuck on roofs, and the general condition of the area.

Jake began to hear horror stories. For example, since the evacuation was not total, many people survived the thirty-foot storm tide by climbing into their second-floor attics, or by knocking out walls and ceiling boards to climb onto their roofs or into nearby trees. People had swum to taller buildings or trees. Over one hundred people were rescued from rooftops and trees in Mississippi. The good news is fewer than three hundred people died in Mississippi during Hurricane Katrina. Jake hoped his family was not included in that number.

Jake decided he would try to make his way back home somehow. He gave up his spot at the shelter and started walking south, open to any idea to get back home that came along. He found out, unfortunately, that all traffic was blocked from going back into the area and there were no means to get there. He met up with some homeless people near a railroad and eagerly partook of some of their whiskey to settle his nerves. Jake was now a homeless alcoholic without support of any kind at the moment to aid his efforts to find his family. He buried himself in whiskey or whatever else he could beg, borrow, or steal. He slept with other nomads around the railroad and drowned his troubles in a bottle.

The Mississippi Gulf Coast had been devastated. The extent of the devastation throughout Mississippi was also staggering. Since Katrina hit, more than half a million people in Mississippi were in the process of applying for assistance from the Federal Emergency Management Agency (FEMA). In a state of just 2.9 million residents, that means more than one in six Mississippians sought help. More than ninety-seven thousand people are today still living in FEMA trailers and mobile homes. Another five thousand to six thousand are still waiting for FEMA trailers.

Surveying the damage the day after Katrina's passing, the Mississippi governor called the scene indescribable, saying "I can only imagine that is what Hiroshima looked like 60 years ago. This is our tsunami."

Most animal shelters in the area were destroyed. Pet enthusiasts developed portable shelters called "Camp Katrinas" to continue their rescue work to save animals.

Cities ran rampant with stray, sick, and malnourished animals. This was true even farther north, where the floodwaters were not so prevalent. One could drive along any street and see five or six dogs in a dead-end street, all looking traumatized and ill. Local authorities saw a growing need to clean up their cities, so they began to pick up the animals en masse every day. Unfortunately, these animals were put down.

Buck, too, was homeless and began his struggles and adventures to find refuge.

Chickens, Voles, and Lyman, Mississippi

Buck hobbled to find a rock formation with an overhang to get under and out of the worst part of the rain. He stayed there for only a little while. He observed the cuts on his paws after climbing onto land. For a long time, he lay on the patch of higher land, licking his cuts and grooming down his thick fur that was covered with mud and water. Buck's big eyes were bloodshot from the water and the stress. He looked rugged and felt exhausted and insecure.

He walked down as far as he could back in the direction of where he had been separated from his master, but he couldn't get a scent on anything as there was so much water everywhere. Not being able to understand what had happened or why, he began to walk among the trees and brush, looking for someone or something to break his thoughts of confusion.

It was still raining hard, but Buck walked for miles and came upon nothing but more trees and brush. He began to feel really lost and abandoned. He would lie down from time to time to rest his sore paws and lick them. Two places were bleeding, and the walking did not help his cuts. At least he was alive.

In northern Harrison County, Mississippi, where Buck was wandering, everything was rural and desolate. Farms and small communities were scattered throughout the county, but the distances between them were great, especially for a walking dog. At nightfall on the first night, Buck crawled under another overhanging rock and tried to make his body as small as possible to break the chill and get out of the rain. It was impossible, however, to stay dry. Mosquitoes and insects were a nuisance; Buck kept biting back at his tail, where the insects would land. He was a very frustrated and unhappy dog at this point. He was dripping wet, hungry, walking with sore paws in the rain, and fighting the insects.

At daybreak he started out again. After about three hours, Buck came upon the outskirts of the small community of Lyman, Mississippi. He saw a house with some smaller buildings around it and headed in that direction. Even though Lyman was only about six miles from where he washed ashore; wandering with no sense of direction in the pouring rain had taken him at least three times that distance.

As Buck got closer to the house, he noticed chickens strutting around the property, and drool began to drip from his mouth. He was really hungry. He had never killed a chicken, but he had chased loose chickens before at home. It was always a game—the chase—the chickens running, and Buck fast on their tails. It had been great fun, and some of those thoughts crossed his mind as he inched closer to the farm.

Buck slinked under the fence and made his way closer to the house, where the chickens were scratching and pecking the ground. He slowly moved in and, at the right moment, took off in a dead run after the chickens. At first he wasn't sure which one to concentrate on, as they were squawking with wings flapping and moving in all directions. It was also so muddy that he skidded down several times. Finally he was able to catch up to a pullet and bring her down.

At this point, he heard dogs barking in the house and a lot of commotion. The screen door to the house opened, and a farmer with his shotgun ran from the house toward Buck and the chickens. Buck felt scared and started to run. The farmer fired the shotgun several times at Buck. Buck was running for his life; he had never heard a shotgun before but knew the farmer's behavior and the sound were not good. As he was running, Buck felt the sting of many shotgun pellets hitting him. He fell once, got up, and continued to run into the nearest clump of trees. He continued to run for almost two miles before he noticed he was no longer being chased by the farmer. Buck had been pelted full of buckshot in his back and legs. He was in pain and found a muddy hole to lie in. Buck felt nauseated and threw up while he was licking his bloody wounds in the muddy water.

The rest of this day was spent hiding in the area; Buck's strength was sapped, and he was starving at this point. As dusk came and Buck lay in the hole, he saw two voles moving ahead of him along the grass.

He gained enough strength to pounce on the area where the voles were. With his nose to the ground, he sniffed out two voles and ate them. He swallowed them whole. Buck would have preferred to kill the voles and eat them more slowly, but he couldn't risk the voles getting away from him. He needed food. It wasn't enough food to make a difference to Buck's stomach, but at least he began to feel a little better after the mini-meal and some success.

Buck was weak, and moving at all caused him pain. Reluctantly, he decided to find a bed for the night. Among the thickets, he felt a little more comfortable, as the rain was not hitting the ground with as much force as before. For the first time, he thought of Ben and the warm bed they shared each night. It seemed a distant memory.

As he lay in the thicket that night, he could hear all kinds of things that kept him alert and wondering. He had never slept outside before now. There seemed to be frequent movement in the thickets of varmints or insects coming out at night. He was tempted many times to forage for food again, but he didn't have the strength or the motivation to hunt in the dark.

From time to time, he could hear trucks and cars on a road in the distance. It was the darkest of darks, and Buck had never been in such a predicament.

Dogs' brains are about equivalent to the brain of a human at the toddler stage. They live for the moment and don't reason or make plans like older children and adults. This was a blessing for Buck during this time of grief, pain, and hunger. He did not think of dying in the same way as we might or wonder what was going to happen tomorrow. He only lay in his den for the night and tried to get as comfortable as possible with all his wounds and sleep a little. He never let his guard down, however, and was ready to jump at a moment's notice.

As light filtered into his den and he listened to the *drip drip* of raindrops falling on his head, Buck woke to a new day. He woke and lay there for a moment, trying to take in where he was and what to do next. He spent the better part of the next hour licking his wounds. The bleeding on his pads had stopped, but they were still tender. He could lick his legs where the shotgun pellets went into his skin, and he could twist around a little to reach a few places on his back. Most of the areas were bleeding. He was even able to chew at one place on his back leg, and one of the pellets came out. The spots were raw and sore. His weak feeling had not changed; he had not had enough food. As he struggled to move in the constant rain, he was reminded of his wounds.

Most people in this predicament would normally be admitted to the hospital for exhaustion, dehydration, near starvation, and treatment of injuries.

Even though Buck had been adopted by the Brown family when he was a pup, he had never been seriously mistreated or needed to fend for himself. However, he had a strong body and an equally strong will. He now had moved from a protected, comfortable life to survival.

Buck was about two years old—luckily still young enough to experience this type of adversity and still have the motivation to move on. He was a beautiful dog of about fifty-five pounds with a thick coat of brindle-colored fur. The thick fur had been helpful to him during the rain, the cold and even the shotgun attack. Buck looked like an Australian cattle dog with the somewhat threatening face of a German shepherd. He was anything but threatening, however, as most people who knew him would tell you. He was adventure-bound, loving, and loyal.

After tending to his wounds, Buck wandered toward the sound of the trucks and cars on the road and soon found himself following the road north for about six blocks into Lyman. Lyman was just a wide place in the road, but it represented the community with a few stores and some commercial activity. It served as home to about 1,100 people and 450 families. Lyman is officially 9.1 miles from Gulfport and 15.2 miles from Biloxi.

As Buck walked slowly toward the cluster of buildings, he saw people coming and going in cars and trucks, entering and exiting the buildings. He saw a few children playing around outside. He also saw two dogs lying on a stoop, looking timid and scared.

Buck decided to sit outside the building where most of the people were going inside. The children began to look at him with wide eyes, noticing the blood on his back and legs and the wet, muddy coat of hair with cockleburs in it. Buck lay down near the door and tried to appear friendlier. One girl came over and touched his head. He licked her hand. She stared at Buck with tears in her eyes and ran inside to tell her mom. The girl's mom came to the door and told her to stay away from the dog, as he could bite because he was injured. Buck looked up at the girl's mom with sad brown eyes, almost pleading for attention. The woman felt so bad for the dog that she went inside to talk to the shop owner. She wanted any meat scraps the man had and bought a box of dry dog food. She asked for a bowl of water. The man was very accommodating, and the woman moved about with a purpose to prepare to help the dog. She was mentally reminded that her family and pets had not been seriously damaged by the hurricane.

The woman came to the door like an angel from heaven with her arms full of food and water. She put it all down for Buck, careful not to touch him. She smiled and gave Buck her best wishes for getting better. She knew she had more important things to take care of at the moment; she couldn't do more. She and her daughter took their bags of groceries and drove away.

Buck ate as if there were no tomorrow. It was several minutes before he even looked up. He noticed that the two dogs from the stoop had crept over near him to watch him eat. He saw the shop owner looking out the window. He looked down at the food left and backed away for the other two dogs to eat. He then lay down nearby and watched them finish the food and water.

After a few minutes, the shop owner came out with a big stick and yelled at the dogs to disappear. He was aggressive in his movements and voice, so the dogs moved on down the street. The two small dogs followed behind Buck as if they had found a leader.

Lady was a blonde Pekingese that had lost her family. The family always tied her to a stake outside when they left the house. For some reason, the family had not returned. When the Hurricane came through, the incredibly high winds lifted Lady off the ground and swung her around the stake in the air. The rope broke, and Lady ran for cover. Hours later, she partnered with a neighbor dog, Teddy, and together they began to wander the area.

Teddy was a brown, black, and white Jack Russell terrier. He was feisty and fast. One wouldn't know that, though, with the way the dog was meandering along behind Buck. Teddy had floated on a rooftop with his family until they were rescued in a boat. The shelter would not take animals, so the parents had told the children Teddy would be better off fending for himself.

Now they were a pack of three very different dogs who shared the same dilemma—homelessness. They felt more comfortable together, but they had little in common as far as personality and appearance. One thing was for sure, though—Buck had become Lady and Teddy's big buddy. He had shared precious food with them: food that he could have kept for himself—food that he could have benefited from after not having eaten for three days. They all seemed to understand the situation; they followed him like a dad with two puppies down the stretch of road. Buck was glad to have company.

Buck was very hot and panting in the humid early September weather. His thick, dark coat held the heat, and his wounds could use some soothing. He led the dogs over to a large puddle of water, where they all lay together. Buck wallowed in the water to get his back covered. Lady and Teddy were not as crazy about being in the muddy water but dutifully stayed near Buck.

Teddy began to chase a honeybee; after eating, he was ready for action. He ran and jumped and tried his best to catch the bee in his mouth. Honeybees are Mississippi's official insect; they are common in the state. The bee was clumsy and gave Teddy a couple of chances, but somehow Teddy never connected. It was all for the better; Teddy didn't realize that he was playing with fire. Buck and Lady watched the entertainment from the cooling pool of water.

Lady had a sore neck from the rope burn that had rubbed off some of the hair on her neck. It was not serious, but she was happy just to rest. She moved closer to Buck, and he licked her neck. They were becoming fast friends. Buck's big pink tongue felt so good on her neck. Lady was a young dog of about ten months old. She liked the comforts of life and missed her family.

Teddy, on the other hand, was a rambunctious young man of one and one half years. He had springs in his feet and could jump as high as the sky. Jack Russells are notorious for their jumping and high energy levels. Teddy lived up to his name and was a cute bag of tricks just waiting to be opened. He lived for the moment and allowed life to be as fun as possible.

Buck decided to hang around Lyman; after all, he had gotten fed here. He kept his gator eyes on the door of the shop where he had eaten. The man had gone back inside, and occasionally someone would drive up and go into the shop. If Buck could avoid the man with the stick, he might get some sympathy from a passer-by—just as had happened before. For the moment, however, his belly was full, and he felt a comfort level come back that gave him more energy.

People would glance over at the three dogs as they entered and exited the area. No one stopped, however, to take a closer look or try to interact with them. Buck wondered if three was a crowd.

In the late afternoon, Buck wandered around the back of the buildings with Lady and Teddy close behind him. There were trash cans and stacks of cardboard boxes behind the shops.

Buck waited nearby until the activity of comings and goings died down. About dusk, when it appeared the shops were closed, he began checking out each trash can.

In the first one, he found oil cans and newspaper. There were several small plastic papers that had the smell of peanut butter on them. He licked them until the peanut butter was gone.

Teddy had already caught on and turned over the second can. He and Lady were sifting through trash, none of which held any food odors. Finally they joined Buck, who was rummaging through the third can, which belonged to the store. They found several pieces of bad fruit and two loaves of stale bread. The three dogs consumed the bread as though it were sirloin steak.

After dinner, Buck headed to the woods for shelter. Teddy and Lady looked at each other like, "Do we want to go into the woods?" and then ran fast to catch up. Buck walked and sniffed around for at least an hour. He ran several squirrels up trees and ended up at a bridge that was nearly covered in rushing water. It was several minutes before Teddy and Lady caught up to Buck. Teddy had stayed longer, chasing the squirrels, and Lady's short little legs just could not go as fast.

This area was officially a swamp. There are many swamps in and around Mississippi. Interspersed with major and minor streams, the large areas of swampland cannot drain, simply because they are as low as or lower than adjacent streams. This is a flood hazard. Over the ages, the land around these flood areas produced rich soil making Mississippi one of the most highly specialized cotton-growing sections of the world.

In the 1700s in this southern area of Mississippi, there were a few tribes of Indians: the Biloxis, Yazoos, and Pascagoulas, all of whom were weaker tribes than the Choctaws in the southeast and the Chickasaws in the north.

Buck crossed the small bridge, perusing the area. After some time, the three dogs came upon a campground area. This was located at the southernmost tip of the Desoto National Forest. The campground is fourteen miles from the Mississippi Gulf Coast, situated adjacent to the Big Biloxi River, where canoeing is a major activity.

Of course, there were no campers. Buck sniffed out all the grills in the campground. He finally decided the place was deserted and harmless. The three dogs bedded down inside the entry area of the restrooms, which had a covered roof. The corner served as a safe spot in which they could remain vigilant to anyone approaching.

Teddy found a spot to himself a few inches away from Buck and Lady. Lady lay close, touching Buck. Buck licked her neck, and Lady was appreciative. She returned the licks to Buck's face. Night and darkness surrounded them as they slept, tired from their day.

About the Author

Shirlee Lawrence Verploegen is currently retired and living in Mt. Juliet, Tennessee, with her two dogs and a foster cat from a Texas raid that captured more than two hundred cats from a hoarding situation. Seventy-nine of those cats came to Tennessee for fostering and adoption. "Being close to nature and enjoying the treasures of retirement with my fur babies makes for a happy camper," she says. She chose a house with some acreage where her dogs can enjoy off-leash exercise and hiking in the woods.

Shirlee has always enjoyed the written word and the beauty of its power. She used her verbal and writing talents in her career as a buyer and then director of retail for a large entertainment company, Gaylord Entertainment Company (part of Opryland Hotel), marketing its brand with retail products and producing phenomenal sales in its retail shops. She established a successful track record for keeping retail under the hotel's umbrella rather than leasing its retail shops to other companies. She retired from Gaylord after twenty-seven years of service.

Shirlee authored and published two coffee-table style resort cookbooks for the company during her tenure that sold fifty thousand copies: *A Taste of Tradition* (1996) and *A Culinary Collection* (2002).

These books containing beautiful pictures of the hotel and featuring favorite recipes from its restaurants are excellent examples of marketing the brand. This was quite a task, as the hotel's kitchen cooked for a three-thousand-room hotel and used very large-scale recipes. Each recipe had to be reduced to family size and tested for excellence.

Shirlee's passion beyond her work has been her love of animals—specifically dogs. She has always volunteered at animal shelters wherever she has lived. She has also done pet therapy with shelter dogs in retirement communities, attended workshops and classes on animal behavior, fostered animals, and done AKC basic obedience training. She was part of the first group to be educated by the Red Cross to learn how to set up pet shelters alongside Red Cross shelters after emergencies. The first Red Cross class coincided with the aftermath of Hurricane Katrina and the resulting vast number of lost pets.

When she lived near a retirement community in Santa Cruz, California, she walked dogs for elderly people and ended up temporarily fostering some of these pups, as their owners would be in and out of the hospital. She was able to research a defunct animal help agency in a deceased woman's will and trace its roots back to the original Santa Cruz shelter and reward the shelter with $92,000. This allowed the shelter to buy much-needed equipment for in-house medical procedures for all animals. This was a shelter that accepted *all* animals. On any given day, it was not unusual to see a horse, pigs, birds, and, of course, lots of bunnies. An interesting tidbit about this particular shelter in this little surf city is that 90 percent of the homeless dogs were either pits or chihuahuas. It was a great shelter that went so far as to offer classes on dog breed behavior, photography, and other fun topics to keep the volunteers on their toes.

In this book's author's notes, the incredible story of the dog Wiggins, the events of which took place after Hurricane Katrina, presents a long-term expression of compassion that ended up with the City of Wiggins, Mississippi, getting a new animal shelter. Shirlee has also written a small children's book about this story titled *Wiggins: A Katrina Love Story*.

You can communicate with Shirlee at shirleeverploegen@facebook.com or shirlee.verploegen@yahoo.com.

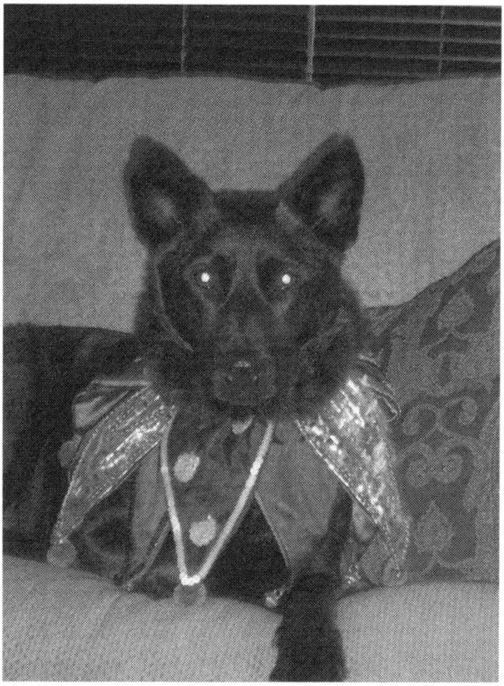

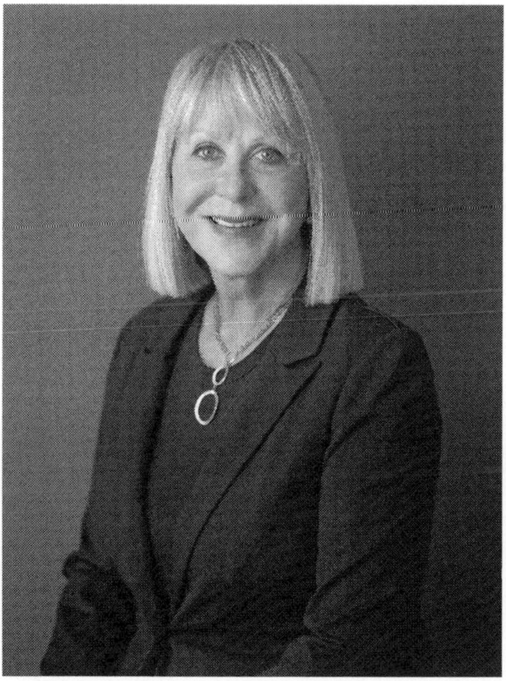

Made in the USA
Coppell, TX
21 February 2020